"She's awake
same."

Nate sipped his soda. "Well, she was in a coma for two weeks. That's gotta affect a person."

"I know. The doctor warned me about that. He said there'd likely be some cognitive impairment. They throw around these big terms like that's how people talk every day. Coordination loss. Muscle regression. Processing difficulties. What he means is, Marnie can't walk or talk right, and she doesn't know who in the world she is. Or who I am, for that matter."

"That's gotta hurt."

"Man, it does. You have no idea. She looks at me like she's looking through me, like I'm invisible. I mean nothing to her. Zip. Nada."

"I'm sorry, buddy."

"I'm not looking for pity."

"But I still feel bad."

"I know you do." Jeff traced a water ring on the table. Like Marnie, he was having a hard time finding the right words. "When she didn't wake up after the accident, I was a mess. I sat by her bed day and night, praying for God to take me instead of her. When she started waking up, I was the happiest guy on earth. But now, when I see her, everything's different. I can tell she doesn't even want me in the room. I'm just an intruder, someone hanging around. When I try to tell her about our life together, she gets this glazed look in her eyes. She doesn't remember a thing. . . . I keep looking in her eyes, looking for Marnie, but she's not there." Jeff snapped his straw between his fingers. "What am I supposed to do, Nate?"

"What do you wanna do?"

"I don't know."

CAROLE GIFT PAGE resides in Southern California with her husband, Bill. This award-winning author of forty-six books once had a job sculpting heads out of clay for a man who made ventriloquist dummies. Today, Carole teaches and speaks at churches and conferences across the country on the topic of "Becoming a Woman of Passion." She and her sister, Susan, a talented singer and ventriloquist, have formed a "Sister Act" and perform often for women's programs and retreats. Susan is accompanied by "Sam," whose head Carole sculpted. Carole also draws from her book *Misty*, about the death of her fourth child—a newborn baby—to share how God can bring us amazing joy in the midst of our deepest sorrows. Carole taught creative writing at Biola University, La Mirada, California, and is on the advisory board of the American Christian Writers. She received the C. S. Lewis Honor Book Award and was a finalist several times for the prestigious Gold Medallion and Campus Life Book-of-the-Year Award. Besides *Misty*, Carole and Bill have three other children—Kimberle, David, and Heather—and four darling grandchildren. If you write to Carole, please include your e-mail address if you would like a personal reply.

Books by Carole Gift Page

HEARTSONG PRESENTS
HP570—Beguiling Masquerade
HP817—By the Beckoning Sea

Don't miss out on any of our super romances. Write to us at the following address for information on our newest releases and club information.

Heartsong Presents Readers' Service
PO Box 721
Uhrichsville, OH 44683

Or visit www.heartsongpresents.com

To Love a Gentle Stranger

Carole Gift Page

Heartsong Presents

To my son, David—my only son! I love you with all my heart and am so proud of you. How thankful I am that you have always walked faithfully with the Lord.

A note from the Author:
I love to hear from my readers! If you would like a reply, please include your e-mail address. You may correspond with me by writing:

Carole Gift Page
Author Relations
PO Box 721
Uhrichsville, OH 44683

ISBN 978-1-60260-284-7

TO LOVE A GENTLE STRANGER

Our mission is to publish and distribute inspirational products offering exceptional value and biblical encouragement to the masses.

PRINTED IN THE U.S.A.

prologue

Hey, my cute little snuggle-bunny, wake up!"

Marnie rolled over and stretched languorously. She wasn't ready to let go of her lovely, pastel dreams. But, as usual, her dear husband wasn't about to let her sleep. "One more minute, Jeff," she pleaded.

"Thirty seconds."

"Forty-five." She pressed one foot against his leg.

"Hey, babe, stop that. Your feet are cold."

"I know. Aren't you my personal foot warmer?"

He raised up on one elbow. "So that's why you married me!"

"That and a million other reasons, Mr. Jordan."

"Really, Mrs. Jordan?" He pulled her into his arms. "I'd love to hear every one."

"It would take a lifetime."

"That's okay." He kissed the top of her head. "I'm yours for a lifetime."

"Me, too." She loved snuggling like this in the mornings—lying in the curve of her husband's arms, her head on his chest, his heart beating against her cheek. It was like being in a warm, safe harbor. Jeff was the kindest, most handsome man she had ever known. And he was hers, all hers. "Jeff, I dreamed about our wedding," she murmured lazily. "We were there on Keauhou Beach under a trellis of plumeria and roses, and the sun had turned the ocean a shimmering gold. Everyone was there cheering us on—our families from the mainland, Nate and Jenny and all our other friends from church and the university. It was perfect."

"That wasn't a dream, honey. That's how it really was."

"I know. Can you believe it's been six whole months? It seems like yesterday. And I was reliving every delicious moment. Until you woke me up!" She sat up, grabbed her pillow, and gave him a playful swat.

"So it's a pillow fight you want? Well, you've met your match!" He seized his pillow and flung it at her. She caught it, but before she could throw it back, he grabbed her around the waist and tickled her.

"Not fair!" she cried between fits of giggles.

"All's fair in love and war! And this is both!"

She wriggled out of his grasp. "Truce! Truce!"

He released her, and they both lay back laughing. She looked over at her smiling husband. His chestnut brown hair was mussed, with several wayward strands curling over his forehead. His blue eyes were twinkling. He reminded her of a mischievous little boy. "Look at us, Jeff, acting like children! I haven't even gotten out of bed yet, and I'm already exhausted."

"Well, catch your breath, babe, because we're driving to Hilo for a day of fun in the sun. I want to be on the road in an hour."

"Fun in the sun? Isn't it always raining in Hilo?"

"I guess you're right. So we'll play in the rain."

She scrambled out of bed. "Speaking of getting wet, last one to the shower fixes breakfast!"

He was right behind her. "I'll fix scrambled eggs if you do the French toast."

"Go put the coffee on, and you've got a deal!"

After breakfast, Jeff opened his thumb-worn Bible for morning devotions. She loved hearing him read the scriptures, but she loved him most when he held her hands across the table and prayed. He had such a natural, spontaneous intimacy with God. Her relationship with the Lord had always seemed more restrained and formal, perhaps because that's how she had been raised. But Jeff was teaching her to relax in God's presence and simply enjoy His fellowship.

The sound of a sudden downpour nearly drowned out their

prayers. Jeff went to the window of their small apartment and looked out. "Can you believe it? It's raining buckets. Maybe we should postpone our trip to Hilo."

She ambled over and hugged his arm. "Come on, Jeff. We won't melt. Besides, we're going to the rainforest where it rains all the time anyway. And we've been planning this trip for days. You know how much I want to see the botanical gardens and Rainbow Falls again. It's where we first kissed, remember?"

"Do you think I could ever forget an amazing event like that?" He jingled his car keys. "Then let's go, babe. Rain or shine, we're on our way."

Minutes later, they were heading along the upper road toward Waimea in their small sedan, affectionately tagged "Old Reliable." Jeff often joked that the car was nearly as old as they were. But it got them where they needed to go. Eventually.

Marnie sighed. "With this rain, it may take all day to get to Hilo."

Jeff leaned forward, white-knuckling the wheel. Traffic was at a standstill. Torrents of water pelted the windshield. "I had planned on getting home early tonight. I have a research paper due for Old Testament Hebrew. It's due Monday."

"Turn around if you like," said Marnie. "I have a paper to write for my journalism class. I guess we'd be better off at home studying."

"But you had your heart set on Rainbow Falls."

"We can go another time, Jeff. Let's just go home, okay?"

"Fine with me."

They were twenty miles short of Waimea when Jeff found a place to turn around on the winding, two-lane road. Traffic was lighter now, but the rain was unrelenting. Jeff glanced over at Marnie. "Sure you don't mind going home?"

She tucked her arm in his. "No, I can't wait to snuggle up on the couch with our laptops."

He laughed. "Now that's a romantic image!"

"You know what I mean. I love studying together."

"And I love our little breaks from studying, when I can steal a few kisses."

She nodded. "That's the best part."

"Totally, babe!"

Marnie stiffened. "Oh, Jeff, be careful!" A truck was approaching on the narrow road, going too fast on the rain-slick pavement. Her hand tightened on his arm.

She watched, transfixed with horror, as the truck hydroplaned across the road into their lane. It bore down on them like a crazed, glassy-eyed behemoth, spewing gravel, out of control. Jeff wrenched his steering wheel to the right. As the truck whizzed by, their vehicle rode the edge of the pavement. Its wheels spun helplessly on the collapsing, mud-soaked shoulder, Marnie's screams mixing with the shrill of squealing tires. With a violent, dizzying shudder, Old Reliable plunged down the steep embankment to the volcanic rocks below. The impact brought convulsive jolts and the shattering, ear-splitting cacophony of metal crushing metal. And then, silence—except for the pelting rain—and utter, all-embracing darkness.

one

Pounding, relentless rain drenched his face, blinding him. He was sandwiched between upholstery and a twisted steel frame. He tried to move. Everything hurt. Tangled metal was everywhere. Something was clamping his leg like a vise. His chest hurt. Hard to breathe. The taste of blood in his mouth, blood and rainwater mixing in his throat, gagging him. He tried turning his head. Couldn't see much with the rain and blood in his eyes. "Marnie?" he rasped. "Marnie, you okay?"

He looked over where the passenger seat had been. It was covered with debris. The windshield was gone. Marnie was lying across the dashboard, her head facedown on the crumpled hood. He wouldn't have known it was Marnie, for all the blood. *She's dead! My baby's dead!*

He stretched his hand out to her, but the world was suddenly spinning, sucking him into a vortex of darkness. From somewhere far away, he heard a siren screaming, or maybe he was the one screaming. He had to stay alert. Had to help the woman he loved. With consciousness ebbing, he fought to stay awake. At last, his eyes closed and his hand fell to his side, while the rain, the screams, and the blood dissolved into blackness.

When he woke, he was lying in a hospital bed, hooked up to tubes and IVs. His parents were sitting beside his bed, looking more worried than he had ever seen them. He tried to talk, but his tongue felt like cotton. His mother got up and leaned over him, touching his cheek with her fingertips. "Jeff, honey, I love you, baby!" Her face looked pinched and her hair grayer than he remembered. She looked older than her fifty-two years.

His father came around to the other side of the bed and

squeezed his shoulder. "Hey boy, you gave us quite a scare!"

"What. . .happened?"

His mother stifled a sob. "You were in an accident, honey."

Jeff forced out the words over the pain in his chest. "How bad. . .is it?"

"You're banged up pretty good," said his father. "Got a cracked rib and torn ligaments in your leg. But, knowing you, you'll be back on your feet in no time."

Jeff managed a crooked grin. "But probably not today, huh?"

"No, not today, son." The lines in his dad's face were deeper, his hair a little thinner, his frame heavier. How long since Jeff had seen his parents? Was it only six months? Yes, they had flown in from California for the wedding last summer.

The wedding. Marnie!

Jeff tried to raise himself up, but his chest hurt too much; he couldn't move his torso. "Where's Marnie?" he cried. "Is she okay?"

His parents exchanged wary glances.

"Mom? Dad? She's okay, isn't she? I gotta see her—now!"

"You can't, honey." His mother ran a cool, soothing hand over his forehead. "She's in surgery, sweetheart."

Jeff's body tightened with alarm. "She's not gonna die, is she?"

"We don't know, son," said his father. "All we can do is pray. And trust God to watch over her."

Jeff sank back and closed his eyes. "Please, God, don't let her die!"

☙

Darkness.

Heavy.

Oppressive.

All-encompassing.

And then, a glimmer of light.

She felt herself rising through layers of blackness toward it, sloughing off fingers of night reluctant to let her go. She opened her eyes to stark whiteness, too bright, nearly painful with brightness. She closed her lids and focused on her own breathing—the ragged intake of air—her chest rising then falling as the air escaped her nostrils. The steady rhythm of her breathing comforted her, although she had no idea why she needed comfort.

She wasn't in pain. Except for the sensation of her own breathing, she wasn't sure she was even connected to her body. She couldn't feel her hands, fingers, legs, toes. She was floating somewhere in space, unfettered by earth.

Was this what it was like to die?

She blinked against the light, slowly adjusting to the brightness. As the physical parameters of the room took shape, her vision swept over foreign pieces of equipment, tubes, and wires—odd contraptions that held no meaning for her—and anonymous paintings of unfamiliar places framed against blank, white walls. Machines whirred and pinged around her with a persistent drone. And the smells assaulting her nostrils were medicinal, sterile, heavily antiseptic.

This isn't heaven!

Then, where am I?

She closed her eyes and waited. It was as if something important had been on the tip of her tongue, at the very edge of her mind, and now it had escaped, had receded from her consciousness into a massive fog bank. She couldn't retrieve it, and yet, she was aware of it, aware of its loss, just as she was aware of a vast store of information—memories, feelings, impressions—stealing away into the murkiness, like a dream that fades on waking, just beyond her grasp.

Her mouth tasted stale, musty, as if she had been asleep for eons. Yes, that was it. She had overslept. That was why she felt so sluggish, so disconnected from her body, her thoughts so jumbled. She tried to move, but her arms and legs refused to respond. How could she have slept so long that she couldn't rouse her own body? It had to be the bed. It was too firm, not her bed. Why was she in someone else's bed?

She heard a voice speaking from a great distance away. A man's voice. Sounding urgent, agitated. "Marnie? Marnie! Thank God, you're awake!"

She stared up into the face of a stranger. He was tall and broad-shouldered, with curly, dark brown hair and thick brows over gentle blue eyes. He was bending over her, his strong hands on her shoulders, his sturdy, chiseled face wet with tears. She opened her mouth to scream, but no sound emerged. The man released her and ran from the room. She sank back against her pillow, her heart hammering.

Just when she thought she was safe, several people—apparitions in white—burst into the room and scurried around her, doing things that made no sense. One woman leaned over her and clasped her hand. "Mrs. Jordan, can you hear me?"

Who's Mrs. Jordan?

The dark-haired man had returned, too. He was touching her face. "Marnie, are you okay?"

At last, she found her voice. "Where. . .am I?" she rasped.

"She's trying to speak," said the man. "That's a good sign, isn't it?"

"Yes," said the woman. "I'll get the doctor."

When she tried to speak again, an incredible exhaustion overtook her, and she felt herself slip back into the soothing darkness.

Sometime later—whether minutes, hours, or days, she had no idea—she woke again and saw the stranger sitting beside her bed. He was reading something—was it a Bible?—and his lanky frame was bent over in the chair as he murmured something under his breath. He appeared to be praying.

Swallowing over the dry, acrid taste in her mouth, she whispered, "What. . .happened?"

The man swiveled in his chair, suddenly alert, and gazed intently at her. The shadow of a beard covered his sculpted chin. "What are you trying to say, Marnie?"

She repeated the words. "What. . .happened?"

"I don't understand. Are you asking about the accident?"

Accident? I don't remember any accident.

"Don't try to talk, Marnie. Just concentrate on getting well."

Getting well? Am I sick? How could I be sick and not know it?

"You. . .my doctor?" she asked, struggling to form the words.

He gave her a look of surprise and incredulity, as if she had asked, *Are you the man in the moon?* "No, Marnie, I'm not your doctor," he said with a slight tremor in his voice. "I'm Jeff. Jeffrey Jordan. Your husband!"

She flinched, fear rising in her throat. *I don't know you! Why are you doing this to me?*

The door opened, and a short, round man with olive skin and small, half-moon eyes entered the room and approached the bed. He asked, "How's our girl doing?"

The stranger said, "She's awake. She tried to speak."

"Excellent." The stout man jotted something on his chart. "For the past few days, she's tracked us with her eyes, but this is the first time she's spoken."

"Her words were slurred, garbled," said the younger man, "but I understood. She thought I was the doctor."

The older man nodded. "Some confusion is to be expected. The fact that she's trying to communicate is a significant step." He pulled a chair over beside the bed, sat down, and took her hand. "Hello, Mrs. Jordan. I'm Dr. Forlani. Can you squeeze my hand? That's it. Keep your eyes open. Look at me, Mrs. Jordan. Stay awake. Squeeze my hand, dear. That's it. Can you squeeze harder? Wonderful." He looked at the young man. "She's following commands. That's a good sign."

The stranger's voice broke with emotion. "Dr. Forlani, you have no idea how hard I've prayed!"

"Yes, I think I do, Mr. Jordan." The doctor lifted her hand. "Can you show me two fingers, Mrs. Jordan? Hold up two fingers, dear. Wake up, Mrs. Jordan. Open your eyes. Can you hear me? Stay with me, dear. . . ."

It had taken every ounce of energy and strength she had to

squeeze the doctor's hand. But she couldn't focus on him any longer. Sleep beckoned—deep, consoling slumber.

When she woke again, the room was shrouded in shadows. The dark-haired stranger was sitting beside her bed, his head back, as if he had dozed off. She turned her head toward him and said hoarsely, "It's. . .dark."

He sat up with a start. "Marnie, you're awake again. Did you say it's dark? It's nighttime, sweetheart." He got up and turned on a light. "There. Is that better?"

She squinted against the brightness. "Who. . .are. . .you?"

His expression fell. "I'm Jeff. Your husband. Don't you remember?"

She shook her head. She wanted to lash out at him for making such an absurd claim, but her body wouldn't cooperate. Her legs felt limp and unresponsive. She was swaddled in coarse blankets and sheets. She could hardly lift her hand.

He reached over and rubbed her bare arm. "It's okay if you don't remember. You've been through a lot. I love you, Marnie."

She flinched. Why did he keep calling her that? "Who. . . is. . .Marnie?"

He flashed a tentative smile. "It's your name. Marnie Jordan."

The name wasn't familiar to her.

He sat back in his chair, eyeing her curiously. "Okay, honey, if you're not Marnie Jordan, then what is your name?"

She closed her eyes to block out the intrusive stranger. Try as she might, she couldn't summon a name for herself. How could it be? She had no idea who she was. She bit her lower lip, fighting back tears. "Go. . .away," she said at last.

The man stood up. "I'll go, Marnie. Just don't get upset. I'll be outside your room if you need me."

A sob tore at her throat. "I don't. . .need. . .anyone!"

The man slipped out the door with a subdued, "I'll be back, honey."

After he had gone, she realized she felt no better, only more confused. She had said, *I don't need anyone.* And it was true. She couldn't picture anyone she knew. She couldn't even summon the image of her own face.

Who am I? And why can't I remember anything?

A nurse—a young honey-skinned woman with short black hair—entered and checked her blood pressure. "Are you feeling better, Mrs. Jordan?"

"I'm not. . .Mrs. Jordan."

The nurse smiled, as if humoring a child. "Dr. Forlani is making his rounds. He'll be in shortly to see you. We're all very pleased that you're awake."

"Where. . .am I?" Suddenly, it was urgent that she know where she was.

"You're in the hospital, Mrs. Jordan."

"What hospital?"

"Kona Community."

"Hawaii?"

"Yes. You live in Hawaii. Remember?"

"No." She tried to move but didn't have the strength. For the first time, she realized she was tethered to an array of tubes and IVs. "A mirror. Please! Get me. . .a mirror!"

"All right, Mrs. Jordan. I'll be right back." The nurse returned a minute later with a mirror and placed it in her hand.

Clasping it with uncertain fingers, she gazed intently at her reflection. The eyes that stared back at her were not familiar. Dark, haunted eyes in an oval face. A full, pale mouth. Porcelain white skin. Tangled, reddish brown hair cascading over lean shoulders. It was a young, almost attractive face, except for the dark circles under the vacant eyes. It was not a face she recognized. She let the mirror fall onto the bed.

"That's not me!" she cried, her agitation growing. "That's not me!"

The nurse patted her arm. "It's okay, Mrs. Jordan. You've been in a coma. It's common to have temporary memory lapses."

She looked up beseechingly. "Coma?"

"The doctor will explain everything to you. My name is Elena. If you need anything, you ask for Elena. Meanwhile, you just relax, Mrs. Jordan. Please, just relax." The nurse turned and bustled out of the room, as if eager to escape.

She was alone again, alone with her muddled hodgepodge of thoughts. She laid her head back on the pillow and tried to steady her breathing. *Something terrible happened to me! Why can't I remember?*

Dr. Forlani entered the room, a chart tucked under his arm. "Hello, Mrs. Jordan. You're looking better this evening."

"I'm not. . .Mrs. Jordan," she murmured under her breath.

"Would you prefer I call you Marnie?"

She carefully enunciated each word. "I. . .don't. . .know. . . her. . .either."

"Then what would you like me to call you?"

She looked away. "I can't. . .remember my name."

Dr. Forlani sat down beside her and smiled. "For a young lady who can't remember her name, you've made a lot of people around here very happy these past few days."

She gave him a begrudging glance. "Why?"

"Because you've returned to the land of the living after a very long sleep."

"How long?"

"Approximately two weeks. But the important question now is, what are we going to do to bring you back to the life you had before the accident?"

She struggled for the right words, her tongue thick in her mouth. "Tell me. . .about the accident."

Dr. Forlani paused a moment then replied, "You were in a car crash, Mrs. Jordan. You sustained a brain injury. You've spent the past several days waking from a coma. And now we need to run some tests to determine how we can best help you recover."

She closed her eyes. The doctor's words were too much for

her. This whole alien world was too painful and overwhelming. *Go away! Leave me alone! I'm not who you think I am! I don't want to be here!* At the moment, all she wanted to do was return to the sweet, soothing oblivion of sleep.

two

When Marnie woke again, the room was filled with sunlight. She noticed two people sitting beside her bed—an older couple in conservative, midwestern-style clothing. Plaid short-sleeved shirt and khaki pants on the man, white blouse and tailored skirt on the woman. They definitely weren't Hawaiians. The woman had short, gray blond hair and delicate features; the man had a weatherworn face and straight brown hair with gray sideburns. Most important, they looked familiar to her.

"Mom? Dad?"

The woman jumped up and rushed to her. "Marnie, oh, sweetheart, you're awake! And you remember us!"

They took turns hugging and kissing her. She wanted to respond with the same enthusiasm, but her thoughts were still jumbled and confused. Almost instinctively, she had acknowledged them as her parents, and yet, her mind fed her no information, no memories or details to confirm such an assumption. She couldn't remember their names or anything about them, except that she knew she shared an enormous emotional bond with them.

The woman sat down beside her and chatted excitedly, speaking so fast Marnie couldn't comprehend what she was saying. "Your dad and I flew in last night from Detroit, Marnie. Long, tiring flight, but at least we made it okay. We were here right after the accident, of course, just as Jeff's parents were here for him. We sat by your bedside for days. Some wonderful people from your church looked after us and made sure we had a place to stay and were well fed. We'll forever be indebted to them. And it was so sweet and touching—some of your girlfriends sat with you and read the Bible and even sang to you.

18

But when over a week went by and you showed no response, we felt we needed to go home and get back to work. You know how your dad's boss is—doesn't want to give him any extra time off. Then, when Jeff phoned yesterday and said you were awake and talking, we were beside ourselves with joy. We immediately made plane reservations, and here we are, dear."

The man stood at the end of the bed, smiling at her with tear-filled eyes. "Marnie girl, you are a sight for sore eyes. We wondered if you'd ever come back to us. I guess the Good Lord was watching over you."

"How are you feeling, sweetheart?" asked the woman. "The doctor says you'll need several weeks of treatment—physical therapy and who knows what all—but everyone's optimistic, honey. You'll be up and walking in no time. Your old self, good as new!"

Marnie laid her head back and closed her eyes. Her mind was shutting down, blocking out the noise, the voices, the chatter that she couldn't quite grasp. "I'm tired," she murmured.

"Of course you are, dear," said the woman. "You've been through a terrible ordeal. We'll go now and let you get some rest."

"If you need anything, honey, let us know," said the man. "We're here for you."

Marnie looked over at the glass of water on her tray. "I want... lightbulb."

"What, dear? A lightbulb? What are you saying?"

"Lightbulb," Marnie said again. What was wrong with them? Didn't they understand that she wanted a drink of water? She nodded toward the glass.

"Water? Is that it, dear?" said her mother. "Why didn't you say so?" She took the glass and put the straw to Marnie's lips. Marnie swallowed the tepid water, but an unsettling feeling gripped her. She hadn't said what she had meant to say. The words were somehow scrambled in her brain. Frustration welled up inside her, but there was nothing she could do to alleviate it.

The shattering truth stunned her. She could no longer speak well enough to express her feelings, her arms and legs had become useless appendages, and she couldn't even trust her mind to feed her the right information. Whoever she was, she was better off dead.

She began to weep.

The woman leaned down and embraced her. "It's going to be okay, Marnie. I know how hard it must be, waking and finding yourself like this. But we're all here for you, sweetheart—your dad and me—and Jeff. He's been by your side every moment. He loves you so much. And all your friends from the university and the dear people from your church—they've been here every day, praying for you and encouraging us. I don't know what we would have done without them. You're fortunate to have so many wonderful people who love you. With their prayers, you're going to get better. I know it, Marnie. Just keep telling yourself that, okay?"

She wanted to scream, *How can I get better when I don't know who I am or who any of you are? I can't even walk or speak correctly! I'm damaged and useless! Why didn't God just let me die?*

Dr. Forlani entered the room and offered his greetings. "How are you today, Mr. and Mrs. Rockwell?"

Rockwell? Is that my name? It doesn't sound familiar. But then, I didn't recognize the name Marnie *either. I'm just starting to get used to people calling me that.*

Dr. Forlani pulled a chair over beside the bed. "And how are you feeling today, Marnie?"

She looked away.

"She's having a little trouble with her words," said the woman.

The doctor nodded. "That's to be expected with a brain injury like this. We'll be bringing in a speech therapist to help her. Did she recognize the two of you?"

"Yes, she seemed to." The woman looked back at Marnie. "You do remember us, dear, don't you?"

Marnie nodded. It was what the woman wanted to hear.

Dr. Forlani checked her pulse. "Are you saying you can recall specific memories from your childhood, Marnie?"

She closed her eyes and scoured her mind for memories. There were none.

"Hey, little girl," said the man, "do you remember when we used to make snowmen in the backyard? You always insisted that we make an entire snow family—the papa with his top hat and cane, mama with a flowered hat and apron, and baby with a rattle and bib. We made their arms with branches from the old oak tree you loved to climb. Don't you remember, baby?" He choked up. Grabbing a handkerchief from his pocket, he wiped his eyes and sniffed. "You always gave them funny names. Mergatroid and Marmaduke for the mama and papa. Sassy Britches for the baby. You loved coming up with crazy names for them. And when the first thaw came and they melted away, you always cried, like you'd lost a good friend. Remember, honey?"

No, no, no! I don't remember.

Dr. Forlani stood up. "Marnie, we're going to let you rest for now. Someone will be coming shortly to help you out of bed. We want to give your legs a chance to regain a little strength. And we'll be running a few more tests. We hope to start your physical therapy this afternoon."

Marnie was glad when the doctor and her parents had gone. As long as she was alone, she didn't have to worry about meeting someone's expectations. She didn't have to pretend to recognize people she didn't know. She relaxed, allowing herself to drift into slumber.

She dreamed. She was rolling a ball of snow across a yard. She could feel the cold through her wet mittens. She could see the little white puffs of vapor in the air as she exhaled. She could taste snowflakes on her tongue. She could hear the crunch of her black rubber boots making footprints in the snowdrifts.

She opened her eyes. *I remember!* The images were broken and disjointed, but at least they were there. Actual memories that belonged to her. She had an identity. It was there somewhere. It wasn't lost forever. She was a real person with a real history. Retrieving it would be like putting a puzzle together. She had the first piece—a little girl in the snow.

She opened her eyes. She needed more of the pieces. "Mom. . . Dad! Where are you?"

A nurse poked her head in the door. "Did you need something, Mrs. Jordan?"

"My. . .parents."

"I'll get them."

The couple returned and sat by her bed. Although she still didn't remember them, she felt their love, and she knew that somehow she loved them, too. "Tell me more. . .about myself."

"Sure, honey," said the man. "What do you want to know?"

"Anything. Everything."

For the next hour, the couple took turns telling her stories— what she was like as a baby, her favorite hobbies and subjects in school, what they did for holidays. Marnie listened intently, creating, piece by piece, an image of herself in her mind.

"You loved making up stories," said the woman. "You pretended there was a family in the attic, and you were always telling us what they were doing."

The man chuckled. "Yeah, lots of kids make up an imaginary friend. You created an entire family."

"Family was very important to you, Marnie," said the woman. "You always wanted brothers and sisters, but we weren't able to have more children. I had several miscarriages. Each time I was pregnant, you got your hopes up. You picked out names and made little drawings for the baby. Losing those children was very painful for your dad and me. But it grieved us even more to see you so heartbroken and disappointed."

Marnie began to weep. "I wanted you to adopt a baby."

"Yes, you did, honey. We checked into it, but we were older. . ."

The man reached for her hand. "Honey, are you saying you remember?"

Marnie's eyes widened. Yes, the memories were clicking into place like video clips on a screen. She remembered her childhood. She remembered her parents! "Mommy!" she sobbed.

The woman—her mother—gathered her into her arms and held her tight. The two rocked together, weeping. Her father embraced her, too. The emotions she felt were delicious, deep, overpowering. She belonged to someone, to these two people who loved her and had known her for her entire life. She wasn't some anonymous soul existing in a vacuum. She was someone's daughter. She was Marnie Rockwell. She had a history and emotional connections. She would survive after all!

three

Hi, Marnie. Your mom says you're remembering things." It was the young man who called himself Jeff or John or something like that. He stood at the end of her hospital bed, his fingers drumming the rail. "Does that mean you remember *us*?" He pointed at himself then at her.

She shook her head. "I don't know you."

He came around, pulled up a straight-back chair, and sat down. "That's okay. They say it'll take time. I'm just glad you're starting to get your memory back. Do you remember anything about Hawaii—about our lives here?"

She glanced out the window at the palm trees and tropical greenery. "No. I remember Michigan. I'm Marnie Rockwell, and I live in Michigan."

"You're Marnie Jordan now. And you did live in Michigan. Several years ago."

"I still do."

"Really? How old do you think you are, Marnie?"

She frowned, struggling to make sense of his question. "I don't know. Am I twelve? Yes, I'm twelve."

"No, honey. You're twenty-two. Like me. You came to Hawaii when you were nineteen." He brushed a shock of curly brown hair back from his forehead. "You've lived here in Kona for three years now."

"Why did I come here?" She was finding it easier to gather her words and form sentences, but what she was hearing left her more confused than ever. "Why Hawaii, so far away?"

"You came here to attend the University of the Nations. Remember?"

"No."

"It's a school where they train people to become missionaries. They're part of YWAM—Youth With A Mission—a cool worldwide mission organization with bases all over the world— in over 160 countries. You know what a missionary is, don't you?"

"Yes." She knew, but she didn't know how she knew. "They tell people about God."

"Right. That's what we want to do, Marnie. Tell people that Jesus died to save them. You remember Jesus, don't you?"

She smiled. Of course she knew about Jesus. " 'Jesus loves me, this I know, for the Bible tells me so.'"

"Yeah, you probably sang that in Sunday school when you were little."

"I don't remember."

"That's okay. You remember Jesus. That's the important thing."

But what did she remember about Him? She had no rational memory of Jesus, and yet she sensed an emotional connection with Him just as she had felt with her parents before she knew who they were.

"Tell me more," she said.

"What do you want to know?"

She shrugged. "I don't know."

"Well, okay, let's see." He shifted in his chair. "We met as students at the university. I'm majoring in biblical studies. You're majoring in journalism and ESL—English as a Second Language. I want to preach. You want to teach people in other countries how to write and publish Christian magazines."

"I want to be a teacher?"

"Right. And you're going to be a great teacher, too. But we've both had to do lots of other things on campus to help pay our way, though most of our support comes from our parents and our churches back home. These days, I do carpentry work and campus maintenance, and you babysit faculty kids. At first, we both worked in the kitchen at U of N. The first time I saw you, you had just dropped a huge bowl of salad on the floor. And you were on your hands and knees scooping up lettuce and tomatoes and carrots and stuff. You looked so flustered and upset. You even got pieces of lettuce and carrots in your hair."

Marnie chuckled. "I'm glad I don't remember that."

"Anyway, you looked so funny and cute. I got down and helped you clean up the mess. I guess you were grateful because you agreed to hang out with me."

She gazed down at her hands. "I don't remember."

"I know."

They were both silent for a long moment.

Jeff craned his neck then scratched the back of his head.

Marnie waited, wishing he would get up and go. It was painful talking with a stranger who knew things about her she didn't know.

He cleared his throat. "I hear they had you up walking today. That's terrific."

She nodded. "I walked down the hall."

"That's great! I wish I'd been here. I had to get back to my classes. Since your folks were here with you, I figured you wouldn't miss me." He paused, his expression darkening. "I guess, since you don't remember me, you wouldn't miss me anyway."

"I'm sorry."

"Don't be. It's not your fault." He sat back and crossed his legs. "Everyone at our church and the university is praying for you. After the accident, they held a prayer meeting just for us."

She stared at him. "You were in the accident, too?"

"Yeah. I was driving the car. I swerved to miss a truck and went over the embankment right into a lava bed."

"Were you hurt?"

"Just some bumps and bruises and a cracked rib. It's okay now."

She nodded. It hadn't occurred to her that anyone else was in the accident.

"It nearly killed me to see you hurt so bad," he said unevenly. "I don't know what I would have done if you. . ." His words trailed off. He swiped at a tear. "I'm just so thankful to God that you're alive, babe."

She recoiled at his words. She wasn't his babe, and she wasn't thankful to be alive. Not like this—without a working mind and body. If she ever prayed again, it would be to die.

"Do you want to hear more?" he asked. "More about our life here in Hawaii?"

"I guess so." She knew already that whatever he said wouldn't mean anything to her. He might as well be talking about complete strangers.

"We're in our third year at the university, Marnie. Our first year, we completed DTS—Discipleship Training School. It's a twelve-week lecture program, followed by an eight-week overseas field assignment. We were both sent to Cambodia. We worked in a teen center in Battambang. We became good friends. By the time we returned to Kona to start our course work for our degrees, we knew we were in love. We got married last summer. We had our wedding on the beach. It was awesome."

Marnie wanted to protest. Surely if she was married to this man, she would remember. How could anyone forget something like that? Maybe he was making up the entire story. Maybe he had fooled everyone, telling people he was her husband. He'd know that with her memory loss, she couldn't contradict him. What kind of man was he—taking advantage of a helpless girl?

"Were my parents there. . .at the wedding?" she asked. They would know the truth.

"Sure. So were mine. We didn't have money for a honeymoon, but we went on a mission trip to Nigeria last summer. We called that our honeymoon. It was amazing. We had a chance to minister to some really neat people. The ladies loved you. You held prayer meetings with them and had a chance to lead several to Christ. You still get e-mails from them, telling how they're growing in the Lord."

Marnie bit her lower lip. She didn't want to hear any more about the woman this eager young man—this John or Jack or Jeffrey, whoever—was talking about. For Marnie, that woman didn't exist.

He pulled a folded piece of paper from his shirt pocket, opened it, and handed it to Marnie. "You got an e-mail just this morning from Nigeria—a girl named Ubong Ibe. I thought you might like to read it."

She glanced down at the paper then thrust it back at Jeffrey. "I can't!"

He set the paper on the nightstand. "That's okay. I'll leave it here. You can read it another time."

She covered her face with her hands. "No! I can't read the words! They're gibberish to me!"

He retrieved the paper. "I'm sorry, Marnie. I didn't know."

She looked imploringly at him. "What's wrong with me? I'm not a real person anymore! I can't even read."

He clasped her hand. "Yes, you are, babe. You hang in there. It'll all come back. You wait and see."

She pulled her hand away. "Go. Please go."

"Not until I've read you Ubong's e-mail. I think it'll cheer you up. It says, 'Dear Sister Jordan, I was very happy to have you as my mentor last summer. We have just come through the most harsh weather of our country—the harmattan season with its dry, cold winds. I read my Bible every day, in good weather and bad. I love you for caring about me. I thank you for helping me know God better. Sorry I don't write often. It's different here. We don't own our own computers. We go to centers away from home. Please write me soon. And remember me in your prayers. Your friend, Ubong Ibe.'"

Tears ran down Marnie's cheeks. "How can I help someone like that when I can't even help myself?"

Jeff's eyes glazed with tears. "I know it's hard, sweetheart. This is the hardest thing you've ever had to do. But you'll get through it. God is with you every moment, and I'll be here for you every day."

She shook her head. "No one can be where I am. Inside my head. Feeling what I feel."

"I know, honey. But give us a chance to try." He folded the

paper and tucked it back in his pocket. "Would you like me to send Ubong an e-mail for you?"

Marnie flexed her fingers. "I can write. My hand is better. Get me a sandwich."

"A sandwich? Are you hungry?"

She scowled. "No, I want to write. Get me a sandwich. And a pen."

"You mean a tablet? Paper?"

"Yes, that's what I said!"

He brought her a pen and tablet from the bureau.

She clutched the pen in her hand. It felt foreign, unnatural. She closed her fingers around it and began to write. The pen slid off the paper. She tried again, pursing her lips tightly. Nothing but chicken scratches! She threw the pen across the room. "I can't write! I can't do anything!"

Jeff reached out to embrace her. She pushed him away. "Leave me alone! Let me die! I want to die!"

He stared at her for a long moment, looking helpless and baffled. Finally, he left the room and returned with a nurse. "Elena, my wife's upset," he explained. "Can you do something to help her?"

The nurse approached her bed. "What's the problem, Mrs. Jordan? What do you need?"

Marnie held out her hands, fingers splayed. "I—I can't read or write!"

"Try to relax, Mrs. Jordan. Lie back and breathe slowly." The nurse picked up Marnie's water glass from her meal tray. "Take a drink of water. You'll feel better."

Marnie knocked the glass from the woman's hand. It flew across the room and shattered against the wall. Marnie buried her face in her pillow. "Go away! Everyone go away!"

❧

Jeff paced the hospital lobby, pummeling his fist against his palm. His stomach was in knots, his head pounding. He had to get out of this place, away somewhere, anywhere. But there was nowhere he could go to erase the image of Marnie looking at him like he was a stranger, worse than a stranger. He pulled his cell phone out of his pocket and punched in a number.

"Hey, Nate, it's me, Jeff. I'm here at the hospital. Where else? You know Marnie's awake now."

"Yeah, that's great news. How is she?"

"She's doing okay, I guess. But listen, I gotta get out of here for a while. With my car totaled, it's kinda hard to get around without imposing on people. I'm looking for new wheels, but the insurance money won't cover much. Would you mind giving me a ride?"

"No problem, bro."

"Really? Great. Pick me up at the front entrance."

A half hour later, Nate Anderson pulled up in his red pickup. Jeff jumped in the cab and buckled his seat belt. "Man, am I glad to see you."

"You okay, buddy?" Nate's ruddy face was pinched with concern.

"Yeah, sure."

"You don't look it."

"Neither do you. New shirt?" The guys were always kidding Nate about his crazy aloha shirts. He was lean as a matchstick, but he sure loved big prints and vivid colors.

"You like my shirt?"

"Looks like an explosion in a paint factory."

"I can get you one just like it."

"Thanks but no thanks."

Nate pulled out of the parking lot. "Where to?"

"You hungry? Wanna go grab a burger?"

"Sure. How about that little place around the corner?"

Jeff waited until they had settled into a booth and placed their order before mentioning Marnie. "She's awake now, you know, but she's not the same."

Nate sipped his soda. "Well, she was in a coma for two weeks. That's gotta affect a person."

"I know. The doctor warned me about that. He said there'd likely be some cognitive impairment. They throw around these big terms like that's how people talk every day. Coordination loss. Muscle regression. Processing difficulties. What he means is, Marnie can't walk or talk right, and she doesn't know who in the world she is. Or who I am, for that matter."

"That's gotta hurt."

"Man, it does. You have no idea. She looks at me like she's looking through me, like I'm invisible. I mean nothing to her. Zip. Nada."

"I'm sorry, buddy."

"I'm not looking for pity."

"But I still feel bad."

"I know you do." Jeff traced a water ring on the table. Like Marnie, he was having a hard time finding the right words. "When she didn't wake up after the accident, I was a mess. I sat by her bed day and night, praying for God to take me instead of her. When she started waking up, I was the happiest guy on earth. But now, when I see her, everything's different. I can tell she doesn't even want me in the room. I'm just an intruder, someone hanging around. When I try to tell her about our life together, she gets this glazed look in her eyes. She doesn't remember a thing. I look at this girl, and I see a helpless, lost little waif. I keep looking in her eyes, looking for Marnie, but she's not there." Jeff snapped his straw between his fingers. "What am I supposed to do, Nate?"

"What do you wanna do?"

"I don't know." The waitress brought them their burgers and fries. Jeff popped a fry into his mouth, but it was too hot. "What if she never comes back to me? What if she stays like this forever? How can I take care of her? What kind of life are we going to have?"

Nate shrugged. "I know it sounds like a cliché, but God can get you through this. He'll give you the strength you need. Hold on to Him, no matter what. And when you can't hold on any longer, He'll still be holding you."

Over the next two weeks, Jeff clung to those words as he juggled his university classes with work and long hours at the hospital. He was at Marnie's side as she began an exhausting regimen of rehabilitation. He encouraged her as she endured the grueling routine of speech, cognitive, and physical therapy. He cheered her on as, like a child, she learned to walk, speak, read, and write again. He pored over every book he could find on brain injuries and amnesia, arming himself with all the information he could get. And even then, he knew it wouldn't be enough.

One afternoon, as he sat in Marnie's hospital room reading, the nurse wheeled her in from a therapy session. It always shocked him to see her again. She looked like a poor imitation of the Marnie he knew and loved—pale, fragile, lost, remote. Even though she was getting better, he still didn't see *his* Marnie in her eyes.

"Well, Mr. Jordan," said the nurse, "your wife did very well today."

He looked up and forced a smile. "A good session, huh, babe?"

She looked down at her clasped hands. "I walk like a two-year-old and read like a five-year-old. And I'm so tired I can't think straight."

Jeff got up and helped the nurse get Marnie out of the wheelchair and into bed. At least—thanks to her mom's suggestion—Marnie was wearing her own pretty pajamas now instead of those ugly hospital gowns.

"You rest now, young lady," said the nurse. "You've had a big day. And don't let her fool you, Mr. Jordan. She's making real progress. One of these days, you're gonna see her skipping down these halls. Nobody's gonna keep her down."

Jeff flashed an appreciative smile. "I'm counting on that, ma'am." He reached over and pulled the covers up around Marnie. It was like tucking in a child. "You're looking good, honey. Even got a little color in your cheeks."

She touched her face. "That's makeup. It's called blush. My mom put it on me this morning. She says I've got to start thinking about my looks."

"You look good to me, no matter what," said Jeff. *Lord, forgive my little white lies.*

"I don't like looking in the mirror," said Marnie, jutting out her lower lip. "It's weird. I don't know that girl."

"Well, I do, and she's pretty awesome." *The old Marnie was awesome.*

She looked over at his book. "What are you reading?"

"This?" He held up the thick textbook. "I'm reading about amnesia."

"So you can figure me out?"

"Something like that." He opened the book and scanned several pages. "Did you know there are several kinds of memory?"

Marnie smoothed the sheet under her chin. "My memory is full of holes."

"But it's getting better," said Jeff. "Listen to this. There's short-term memory, like remembering where you put your car keys. And there's long-term memory—remembering what happened years ago. There's episodic memory. That means you remember your own experiences. And there's semantic memory—storing facts about history and stuff."

She put her hands over her ears. "I don't want to hear it. It doesn't make sense to me."

"Okay. How about this? There are two types of amnesia. Anterograde amnesia means you remember the past but can't form new memories. Retrograde amnesia means you've forgotten what happened before your injury."

"I remember Michigan, when I was a little girl."

"But not Hawaii, right?"

"I don't remember Hawaii."

He tried to keep his voice steady, nonchalant. "Which means

you still don't remember anything about us."

She shook her head.

"That's no good." He looked back at the book, fighting the taste of disappointment in his throat. "I think you have both kinds of amnesia, because you forget things now."

"What things?"

"My name. Do you remember my name?"

"John?"

"Jeff!" He hated it when she did that, calling him some other guy's name. "What day is it, Marnie?"

"I don't know."

"What month?"

"Summer? The sun is shining."

He sighed. "It's February. The accident happened in January." He wasn't ready to give up yet. "What did you have for breakfast?"

"I don't know. Did I have breakfast?"

"You had cereal with bananas and milk. And orange juice and toast."

She scowled. "How do you know?"

"I was there."

She rolled over and buried her face in her pillow. "I don't like this game. Go away."

Jeff sat back and shook his head. *What's the use? It's hopeless! I can't get through to her.*

The door opened just then, and Marnie's mother peeked inside. "Is this a private party, or is everyone invited?"

Jeff got up and opened the door wide, relief sweeping over him. Reinforcements! "I don't know about everyone, Barbara, but you're sure welcome." He pulled over the comfortable, overstuffed chair for her. "Sit down. Spend some time with your daughter. I'll go for a little walk."

"You don't have to leave, Jeff."

He headed for the door, his book tucked under his arm. "No, that's okay. You two ladies need some private time together.

I have some work to do at the library."

Marnie's mother nodded. Her face looked weary, strained. "Okay, Jeff, if you insist."

He was out of there before anyone could say another word. *Gotta get away. Gotta get out of here. Gotta clear my head and catch my breath.* As he strode down the hospital corridor, guilt stabbed him. What kind of husband was he? He couldn't get away from Marnie fast enough. She was the love of his life; yet at times, he could hardly stand to be in the same room with her.

🌿

Marnie watched in silence as the young man named Jeff or John left the room and shut the door behind him. She was glad he was gone. He made her nervous with his incessant questions. Always wanting to know how she was. Did she remember this or that? Always talking, telling her stories that meant nothing to her.

"Marnie, dear, I have a surprise for you." Her mother sat down beside her and smiled.

"I like surprises."

"Good. Because I brought along some scissors, rollers, and mousse. I thought it was time for you to have a nice hairstyle again."

Marnie put her hands on her head. "My hair's fine."

Her mother ran her fingers through the long strands. "The Marnie I know wouldn't let anyone see her with hair like this."

Marnie pushed her mother's hand away. "I don't know that Marnie!"

Her mother clasped her arm. "I'm sorry, sweetheart. I shouldn't have said that. I just thought you might like to have pretty hair again. We couldn't do much with your hair before, because of the bandage."

"What bandage?"

"You know, honey. Where they put the catheter in your head to relieve the swelling."

"I don't remember."

"There's a word for it. A whopper of a word. Ventri—ventriculostomy. It saved your life, honey. The doctor told us most damage comes not from the original injury, but from the brain swelling during the first week. We're very fortunate to have doctors who knew just what to do to help you."

Marnie pointed at the little cloth bag her mother was holding. "What's that?"

Her mother handed her the bag. "These are the rollers I'm going to put in your hair. They'll make your hair look pretty."

Marnie removed several plastic rollers and stuck them in her hair. She shook her head, but they held firm. She started to laugh. "Now I'm pretty!"

Her father entered just then and grinned at her. "Well, look at my girl with a head full of curlers!"

"Am I pretty, Daddy?"

"The most beautiful girl in the world, sweetheart."

"But the point isn't to wear the curlers, but to wrap your hair around them," said her mother, pulling a curler from Marnie's tangled hair.

"No, I like them like this!" said Marnie.

Her mother removed a brush from her purse and began brushing Marnie's hair. "Do you remember what I called the snarls in your hair when you were little?"

Marnie thought a moment. "Rats! You said I had rats in my hair."

Her mother beamed. "That's right. That's exactly what I called them."

"See? I remember."

"And you'll be remembering more all the time, honey."

"That's what that boy says, too."

"Boy?"

"The one who's always here. Jack?"

"Jeff."

"Right. He's always here."

"Because he loves you, sweetheart."

"He bugs me."

"Why?"

"I don't know. He just does."

Her father came around and put his hand on her mother's shoulder. "Have you told her yet?"

"Not yet. I was waiting for you."

"Leave the dirty work for me," he murmured under his breath.

"I just thought we should tell her together."

"Tell me what? Is it a secret?" asked Marnie. "A riddle?"

"No, dear," said her mother. "It's time for your dad and me—"

"What your mother's trying to say is, we've been away from home a long time, Marnie. Weeks now. And we both have jobs to get back to."

"The thing is, Marnie, your dad and I are flying home to Michigan tomorrow."

She stared from one to the other. "No, don't go!"

"I can't take any more time off from work, sweetheart," said her father, his eyes tearing.

"I want to go to Michigan, too."

"You can't, honey. You're right in the middle of your rehabilitation program. You need to stay here and get better."

She clutched her mother's arm. "Take me, too. Please, Mommy!"

Her mother pressed Marnie's hand against her cheek. "We can't, honey. You need special care. Care your dad and I can't give you."

"Yes, you can. I'm your little girl. I'll be good!"

Tears streamed from her mother's eyes. "Oh, honey, of course you're good. You're our beautiful, wonderful daughter. But you need to stay here and get well."

"If I get well, can I come home?"

Her father sidled over and rubbed the back of her neck. "You will go home soon, honey. To your home with Jeff. He's so eager for you to come home."

Marnie scowled. "I don't know him. I don't like him."

"He's your husband, Marnie," said her mother. "You promised to love him always."

"I love you and Daddy. I'm your little girl."

Her father kissed the top of her head. "You'll always be our little girl. But you're also Jeff's wife, and you belong with him."

Marnie began to weep. "Take me with you. Please! Pretty please! Take me with you!"

"We want you to get your life back, honey. We want you to be whole again. That won't happen if you go back to being our little girl. Give Jeff a chance to show you how much he loves you."

"No, no, no!"

Amid her tears, they took turns hugging and kissing her good-bye. As they left the room, she pounded her tray with a spoon, screaming, "Mommy! Daddy! Don't go! Don't leave me!"

four

Jeff paced the floor outside Marnie's hospital room, waiting for her to dress and pack up her things. It was exactly two months since the day of the accident, and she was being released today into his care. She would continue her therapy as an outpatient, but he would be the one taking care of her now. He wasn't sure he was up for the job. And he knew Marnie wasn't eager to go home with him. He couldn't blame her. She still didn't have a clue who he was. Well, that wasn't true. She had been told often enough that he was her husband, but it didn't sink in. She didn't believe it in her heart of hearts.

The nurse appeared with a wheelchair. "Your wife is all checked out, Mr. Jordan. I'll get her, and you can be on your way. I know this has to be a wonderful day for the two of you."

"Yeah, Elena, it sure is." Guilt nudged him. Sure, this should be one of the happiest days of his life. He was taking Marnie home. Then, why was he scared out of his wits? Why would he rather be almost anywhere else?

"We're ready, Mr. Jordan." Elena squeezed his hand as she handed him a plastic hospital bag of Marnie's things. "I just want you to know, I said a lot of prayers for the two of you. And I know so many of your friends have been here every day praying. God answered our prayers. I know you're going to have a wonderful life together."

"Thanks. Everyone's been so supportive—our family and friends, the doctors and nurses. We appreciate everything." He couldn't think of what else to say, so he simply followed the nurse as she wheeled Marnie out to the car. He helped her into the passenger seat and tossed her things into the backseat. Marnie looked almost like herself in her green knit top and denim capris. It felt strange, like he was taking someone home who looked like Marnie but was really someone he hadn't quite gotten to know yet.

"Am I well?" she kept asking as he headed back to their apartment near the university.

"You're getting there, honey." He always had to couch his replies in simple, positive words, as if he were answering a child. "You're a hundred percent better than you were a month ago."

"Will I go back to the hospital?"

"Yeah, but you won't sleep there. You'll go three days a week for your therapy sessions."

"Where will I sleep?"

"At our place."

"Where are we going?"

"Home."

"To Michigan?"

He sighed. Would she ever get over the idea that she belonged in Michigan? "No, not Michigan. To our apartment. You'll like it. Why wouldn't you? You decorated it. Most everything in the place is your stuff, except for my favorite beanbag chair and my sports trophies."

"Sports trophies?"

"Yeah. I ran track. I was the fastest runner in my high school. Six years later, my record still stands for the hundred meters." *Why am I rattling on like this? I'm going to overwhelm her. Why can't I just shut up!*

"Where did you go to high school?"

"California. Burbank. It's where I was born and raised."

"Oh." She gazed out the window at the passing scenery. "Are we there yet?"

"Getting there." He was miffed. She wasn't listening to him. She was like a little kid. Distracted, impatient. There had to be something they could talk about, something to engage her attention. "How do you like our new car?"

"It's new?"

"Actually, it's eight years old. But I got a great deal on it. We needed another car. Old Reliable was totaled in the accident."

She gave him a bewildered glance. "Old who?"

"Old Reliable." Why would he think she'd remember that when she had forgotten everything else? "It's the nickname we gave our car. I know it sounds dumb, but the old rattletrap was sort of like a member of our family."

"I like a car with a name."

"Me, too."

"What is this car called?"

He gave her a quick smile. "I haven't named it yet. I was waiting for you to help me."

She crossed her arms on her chest. "I'm not good at names. I can't even remember yours."

"Jeff."

"And I'm Marnie."

"Right. See, you're getting it."

"I am?"

"I bet you'll come up with the perfect name for this hunk of metal." He turned onto Kuakini Highway. He had an idea, the perfect thing to stir her memory. "Would you like to see where we go to school?"

She shrugged. "Whatever."

"It's a beautiful campus. Forty-five acres. It looks out over Kailua Bay. You can stand on the campus and look out at the ocean and see cruise ships in the harbor. The sunsets are breathtaking."

She tugged on his arm. "John, I'm hungry."

"Jeff." He saw red every time she called him the wrong name. Why was it so hard to get a simple name right?

"I'm hungry, Jeff."

"We could grab a burger at a fast-food place."

"I want macaroni and cheese."

"You hate macaroni and cheese."

"I love it."

"You ate it at the hospital all the time, but before that, you hated the stuff. You'd make it for me once in a while, but you never ate any of it."

"I want macaroni and cheese."

"Okay, we'll fix some when we get home. But it'll be out of a box."

She smiled. "I'd love a box of macaroni and cheese."

"But first, I want you to see the university. Maybe it'll jog your memory." He made a left turn onto the campus. *Lord, please let her recognize something. Let me know the old Marnie is still in there somewhere.* "See those buildings over there on the right?"

"I guess so."

"See the sign with the red 'Aloha' on it? That's the Visitors Center. Next is the Global Outreach Center." They passed a row of umber brown, two-story buildings. "Keep watching, Marnie. See that circle of flags with the fountain in the center? That's the Plaza of the Nations. Those are the national flags of all the students on campus. And the stepping-stones around the fountain were gathered from every nation on earth. Cool, huh?"

Marnie slumped down in her seat. "I'm tired, Jack."

"Jeff," he muttered. His hopes were nose-diving like paper airplanes in a downdraft. "Do you remember any of it, Marnie? Anything at all?"

"No." She laid her head back and closed her eyes. "I should go back to the hospital. My bed is there."

"We're not going back to the hospital. We're going home, Marnie. To our apartment. Right now!" His sudden anger surprised him. Where did it come from? This was supposed to be a happy day. Marnie couldn't help it that she wasn't herself. *Lord, help me! Don't let me spoil this day just because it's not the way I wanted it.* He turned the car around and headed back to Kuakini Highway. "Our apartment is just on the other side of the highway. We'll be there before you know it."

❧

Marnie couldn't stifle her feeling of dread. It had been growing steadily, spreading through every cell of her body, making her palms sweat and her heart pound harder. She had been away from the hospital for less than an hour, and already, she wanted to go back. Everything about it was familiar. Everything in this new world was strange. She recognized nothing. And she had no desire to get acquainted with it. What little independence she had managed to achieve at the hospital was slipping away. The familiar white room, the daily routine, and people who took care of her were gone now. She had no idea what to expect next.

She watched in wary silence as the man who called himself her husband pulled into a parking lot beside a tan, two-story building with a red tile roof. It was an attractive complex surrounded by towering palms and lush, tropical greenery, but it looked no more familiar than the far side of the world.

"Not bad, huh, Marnie? There's even a courtyard with a pool," the man—her husband—said as he helped her out of the car. "We could go swimming later. It would help get the strength back in your legs."

She hugged her arms to her chest. "I don't know how to swim."

"Yes, you do. You're a better swimmer than I am."

"I am?"

"You wait and see. Swimming is like riding a bike. You never forget how."

"I had a bike. I remember riding my bike." The memory helped soothe her dread.

"Well, you keep those memories coming, babe." He led her up the walk to the nearest unit and unlocked the door. "Good thing we have a downstairs apartment. No steps to climb." He pushed the door open and moved aside. "Go on in, hon. It's been waiting for you for a long time."

She held back. "You go."

He took her hand and led her inside. Something in his face changed. His voice filled with emotion. "Wow! This brings back memories, seeing you in this room again. I almost feel like I should carry you over the threshold or something."

She gave him a puzzled glance. "Why? I can walk."

"Never mind." He released her hand and opened the blinds, letting the sunlight in. She looked around. This wasn't so bad. Nothing scary or threatening. The room was cozy and inviting, with wicker furniture and a red tile floor with white throw rugs. At the far end of the room was a small kitchen with a glass-top table and wicker chairs.

"Do you recognize it?" he asked.

"No, but it's pretty."

"You lived here for six months."

She ambled into the kitchen and ran her hand over the granite countertop. It felt smooth and cold. She lifted the top off a ceramic cookie jar shaped like a fat brown bear.

"No cookies," he said. "That was your department. You always baked those chocolate chip cookies that come in a tube."

"Cookies in a tube?"

"Yep. We'll make them sometime. Assuming you still like cookies."

"I love cookies."

"Good. Me, too." He went over to the refrigerator and opened the door. "See all these casseroles? We have plenty to eat. The ladies at church have been keeping me well fed."

"Is there macaroni and cheese?"

"No, there's chicken and rice, ham and scalloped potatoes, meat loaf—"

"I want macaroni and cheese."

He shrugged. "Okay, there's probably a box in the cupboard."

She looked around. "Where's the bedroom?"

"I'll show you." He walked to the end of the hall and opened a door. She followed him inside. It was a small room with shuttered windows, a double bed, small glass lamp stands, and a ceiling fan that looked like palm leaves. "Your clothes are in the closet and drawers," he told her. "Do you want to rest while I fix lunch?"

She studied the oak bureau for a moment then tentatively pulled open a drawer. It was filled with a man's clothing.

"That's my drawer," he said. "You have the top three; I have the bottom three."

She nodded and tried another one. It contained lingerie and undergarments. She quickly closed the drawer.

Jeff rubbed the back of his neck. "I'll leave you alone while you settle in." He started out the door then paused and looked back at her. "Just so you know. I set up a cot in the other bedroom. I figured that's the way you would want it for now."

Relief swept over her. "Thank you." She sat down on the bed and bounced a little. "I like this. It's softer than my other bed."

"Yeah. We always thought it was pretty comfortable." He gave her a little wave and headed out the door. "Guess I'd better get busy on that macaroni and cheese."

She was quickly on his heels. "I'll help you, Jack." She wasn't ready yet to be left alone in this strange new place.

"Great. Come on."

He got a box out of the cupboard and handed it to her. "You open this while I get a pan and start the water boiling."

She pulled at the box, but her fingers wouldn't work right. Infuriated, she tried several more times to open it then gave up and slammed the box against the countertop. It broke open, and dry macaroni flew everywhere.

"Way to go, Marnie!" Jeff turned off the spigot and set down the iron kettle he was filling. He sounded frustrated, too. "There goes our lunch!"

She began to cry. She didn't want to be here. She didn't want any of this, and yet, here she was, forced to do things that had nothing to do with her. And it was all going badly, just as she had feared.

"It's okay, babe." Jeff gave her a quick hug. Without emotion, she accepted the embrace, her arms at her sides. "No use crying over spilled macaroni. We'll try one of those casseroles."

After Marnie nixed the casseroles, they ended up eating peanut butter and jelly sandwiches. She loved them. When she had finished her sandwich, she stuck her finger in the jar, scooped out a gob of peanut butter, and licked it off her finger. "This is so good!"

"Better drink a lot of milk with that, or it'll get stuck in your throat." He refilled her glass. "There. Wash it down with that."

She drained the glass.

"Hold on," he said. "We forgot to pray."

"We did?"

"Yeah, we always say grace before meals. It's been so long since we've sat together at our table like this I completely forgot to ask God's blessing." He reached across the table and took her hands. "We have so much to be thankful for, babe. God brought you back to me. There were times when I didn't think the two of us would ever be here like this again."

He bowed his head and began praying. Marnie began to hum. She hummed the entire time he was praying. After he had said, "Amen," he looked up at her and asked, "What was that all about?"

She looked puzzled. "What?"

"The humming. Why were you humming?"

"I like to hum."

"But not while I'm praying."

"Why not, Jack? God doesn't like humming?"

"I don't know if He does or not. It's just not polite to hum when someone's praying."

"I could hum with words. We did that in the hospital sometimes, remember? People came and sang to me. You sang, too."

"We were singing praise songs, Marnie. That's different."

"Why?" She sensed she had displeased him.

"I don't know. It just is."

He got up and started clearing the dishes. "You know, you

can pray whenever you want, Marnie. I used to love to hear you pray."

"I don't think so." Why did he keep asking her to do things she didn't know how to do?

"Why not?"

"I don't remember what to say."

"Just say whatever's on your heart. Whatever comes to mind."

"I'll pray later."

"You don't have to pray out loud. You can talk to God anytime in your thoughts. Just you and God."

She twirled her milk glass between her palms. "He's listening in, isn't He?"

Jeff filled the sink with soapy water. "He's with us every minute, hon. He never leaves us."

"Or forsakes us."

"Right. That was one of your favorite verses." He put the plates in the sink. "Would you like me to read you some more verses?"

Marnie got up from the table and looked toward the door. "Is it time to go back to the hospital?"

Jeff took her glass and washed off the table. "No, hon, not until tomorrow."

Her shoulders sagged. "How long is that?"

"About nineteen hours before your physical therapy."

"I should get ready."

"You'll have plenty of time to get ready tomorrow morning."

"What about my hair?"

"What about it?"

"My mom puts my hair in rollers."

Jeff laughed. "Yeah, I remember how you looked in those rollers in the hospital. But I don't think you use rollers, Marnie. I've seen you using a flat iron or a curling iron."

"I iron my hair?"

"Yeah, I guess you could call it that. Come to the bathroom. I'll show you what I'm talking about."

She followed him into the bathroom. He took two appliances out of the cabinet. "See these? One makes your hair straight, and the other makes it curly."

"That's confusing. Which way should it be, Jack? Straight or curly?"

"Either way. It's your choice."

She held the two irons, one in each hand, trying to decide what to do. She sensed that this was an important thing to know. It held the secret to pretty hair. She looked up at him. "Show me how to work them, Jack. Pretty please."

He chuckled. "Sure, babe. And, by the way, it's Jeff. But I guess you won't remember that two minutes from now anyway." He plugged in the flat iron and turned it on. "We've got to wait a few minutes for it to get hot. When it does, be careful, because it gets superhot. Like a stove, you know? Don't burn yourself."

"I won't. There's no fire."

"You don't need flames to get burned. Maybe you should let me do it for you."

"No, Jack. I can do it."

"Jeff."

"I can do it, Jeff. Just show me how."

"Okay, now that it's hot, you take the flat iron, put a small section of hair in it, and pull it all the way down to the end. There. See? Now it's straight." He took another section and clamped the iron down on it. "Now you try it."

The phone rang in the living room. "I'll get that. You practice, okay?"

She forced herself to remain stone still while the flat iron did its work. She held her breath, waiting, wondering how long it would take. *I can do this. I can take care of myself. I can do it!* She smelled something hot. It was working, making her hair straight, making it pretty. The iron began to smoke. Something wasn't right. She opened the tongs, and a tuft of singed hair fell into her hand. She dropped the iron. It clattered on the counter.

She let out a shrill scream and ran out of the bathroom, still clutching the tuft of scorched hair.

❧

Jeff was on the phone. It was Marnie's mother, the last person on earth he wanted to talk to right now. So far, the day had been a comedy of errors. Or maybe *tragedy* was a better word. The way things were going, Marnie's parents would be whisking her off to Michigan in no time flat. And maybe that wasn't such a bad idea after all—if today was any example.

"That's right, Barbara," he replied calmly, even though he heard a commotion in the bathroom. "Everything's, uh, going great. Your daughter's settling in just fine. Um, yeah, that was Marnie screaming, but it's okay." He turned around and looked at his distraught wife, standing there, bawling like a baby, a bunch of burned hair in her hand. "She's just a little upset about her hair. Can we call you back in a few minutes? Thanks. Bye."

Marnie waved the clump of hair in his face. "It didn't work!"

He drew her into his arms and gave her a comforting embrace. "I'm sorry, honey. Don't be upset. Give yourself time. You'll get the hang of it."

Between sobs, she lamented, "I can't do anything right!"

He kissed the top of her head and murmured, "You're still beautiful to me."

She stopped crying and tried to pull away. His arms tightened around her. Holding her like this brought back all the old feelings, the closeness they had shared, the yearnings, the sweet intimacies. This was his wife, the woman he loved like no other. At last, she was in his arms again. "Please, Marnie, it's been so long. . . ."

She placed her hands against his chest and gave him a hard shove.

He stumbled backward and caught himself. "What'd you do that for?"

"You wouldn't let go." With her singed hair still in her hand, she ran to the bedroom and slammed the door behind her.

Jeff dropped down on the sofa and put his head in his hands. It was only Marnie's first day home, and he was already at the end of his rope. Was he wrong to have brought her home? Was there anything left of their relationship? He had promised to love and cherish this woman for the rest of his life. But nothing had prepared him for a situation like this. *Lord, Lord, where do we go from here?*

five

When Marnie woke the next morning, she was still wearing yesterday's denim capris and knit top. She rolled over and hugged her pillow. Something wasn't right. This wasn't the hospital. She was in a strange place. It felt different, smelled different. She sat up and looked around the room. It was someone's bedroom. Slowly the details clicked into place. This was where that man Jack lived—the man who claimed to be her husband. He had insisted it was her home, too, but she didn't really believe him. He said a lot of things that she just let fly over her head because they made no sense to her.

She swung her legs off the bed and planted her feet on the cold, hardwood floor. She drew her feet back up, curling her toes. There was something she was supposed to do today. Someplace she was supposed to go.

The hospital! Of course! They were helping her learn to read and write again, and get her strength back. It was a good place. Except for scattered memories of her life in Michigan with her parents, her only memories were of the hospital and her new friends there—the doctors, nurses, technicians, and therapists.

And then there was Jack. He was always hanging around.

She got up and went to the bathroom. The flat iron and curling iron were still there on the counter. She stared at herself in the mirror. No matter how many times she looked at her reflection, she was always surprised to see someone she didn't recognize. She ran her fingers through her long, auburn brown hair. Maybe no one would notice that a clump of hair was missing.

She ambled out to the kitchen where Jack or Jeff or whoever was standing at the stove, cooking something. He looked at her and smiled. "Good morning, sleepyhead. I was wondering if

51

I was going to have to come wake you up. You've got to be at the hospital in an hour."

"I'm ready," she said.

He laughed. "I don't think so. Did you sleep in those clothes?"

She nodded.

"You have nightgowns and pajamas in the drawer."

She looked down at her capris and top. "I like these."

"You can't wear them to the hospital."

"Yes, I can."

He shook his head. "The old Marnie wouldn't wear something she had slept in."

She shrugged. "I don't care. She isn't here."

"You can say that again." He flipped a pancake on the griddle. "Are you hungry?"

"Yes. I love pancakes."

"Good. I made plenty."

She watched as he poured the batter. "I like pancakes like my mother makes. She makes little animals, with heads and legs and tails."

"Sorry, babe. I just make circles." He set a stack of hotcakes on the table then took syrup and butter from the refrigerator. "Sit down. Help yourself."

She sat down and looked at her plate. "I like sour cream on my pancakes."

He put a pitcher of orange juice on the table. "Really? Sour cream?"

"Yes. Sour cream."

"Are you sure you don't mean whipped cream?"

"Yes! Whipped cream."

He sat down and filled their glasses with juice. "Sorry, honey. We have lots of casseroles, but we're out of whipped cream. The church ladies kept me fed, so I haven't done much grocery shopping since you've been gone. Besides, you were the one who always knew what we needed."

"We need whipped cream."

"We'll go shopping after your therapy session today. Okay? You can buy whatever you like." He reached across the table for her hand. "Let's say grace before we forget again, okay?"

"Okay." She bowed her head and closed her eyes.

"How about you praying this time, Marnie?"

She looked up. "Me? I can't."

"Sure you can. Just say whatever's on your heart."

She closed her eyes again and gnawed her lower lip. Finally, in a small voice, she said, "Hi, God. It's me. Marnie Rockwell. I like pancakes, even if they're not little animals like my mother makes. Thank You for the pancakes. Amen."

"That's great, Marnie, even though you're actually Marnie Jordan now. I bet God loved that prayer." He helped her spread butter on her hotcakes then handed her the syrup. She held the open bottle over her plate until the pancakes were swimming. "That's enough, Marnie. Save some for me."

She tried cutting her hotcakes. When that didn't work, she speared one on her fork and tried eating it whole. That didn't work, either.

"Here, babe, let me help." Jeff reached over with his knife and fork and cut the stack into bite-size pieces.

When they had finished eating, he asked, "How were the pancakes?"

"They were boring little circles," she replied. "But they tasted good."

He sighed. "You win. Next time, we make little animals." He got up and carried their dishes over to the sink. "Why don't you go take a shower while I clean up the kitchen?"

"Okay." She got up and headed for the bathroom, but once inside, she stared blankly at the shower fixtures. How did the water come out? She turned one handle, but when nothing happened, she pulled another. Still, no water. She went to the doorway and called, "Jack, there's no water!"

He came sauntering down the hall, wiping his hands on a dish towel. "You can't turn the water on?"

"No, it won't work."

He stepped into the shower. "You've got to turn on the faucet. This one's hot; this one's cold."

"Like this?" She reached in and turned the handle. A geyser of cold water shot out.

Drenched, Jeff stumbled out, wiping water from his eyes. "Why'd you go and do that?"

Marnie broke into laughter. "You're all wet, Jack. You look so funny!"

"It's not funny, Marnie." He towel dried his hair. "Now, I've got to go change." Suddenly, he grabbed her and pulled her against him. "There! Now you're wet, too."

She wriggled out of his grasp, stepped back, and ran her hand over her damp shirt. "It's okay if I'm all wet. I'm taking a shower anyway."

"Yeah? You can't take a shower with your clothes on."

"I know. I'll take these things off."

Jeff looked away. "There's a robe in the closet. While you're at it, find something suitable to put on for your therapy session."

A half hour later, Marnie stepped out of the bathroom, showered and dressed. "I'm ready," she told Jeff.

He was busy putting away the last of the dishes and didn't pay any attention to her at first. When he finally looked up, he did a double take. "What are you wearing, Marnie?"

"Clothes."

"You're wearing *my* clothes. My plaid flannel shirt and my black corduroy pants! You can't wear them!"

"Why not? I like them."

"First of all, they're for a man. And they're way too big on you."

"Girls wear big shirts. They're in style."

"Maybe ten years ago, but not now. Why didn't you pick something from *your* side of the closet?"

"I didn't like anything."

He took her hand and led her to the bedroom. He slid open the door to her side of the closet. "Now, pick out something to wear. If you want me to, I'll pick something for you."

She gave him a pouting glance. "You pick. I can't decide."

He grabbed a pair of patch-pocket jeans and a green pullover shirt. "Put these on, Marnie. You like green. Come on. We've got to get going."

Neither of them spoke during the drive to the hospital. She was glad when he dropped her off and went on to his classes at the university after promising to pick her up after her therapy. If there was anything worse than living under the same roof with a stranger, it was living with a grouchy stranger. She had been too proud to admit she had no idea how to find the rehabilitation department, but after wandering the hospital corridors for a long while, she encountered a kind nurse named Elena who showed her the way.

That afternoon, when she was finished with her therapy sessions, she found Jeff waiting to take her home. As he walked her to the car, he said, "I'm sorry I got mad at you this morning. Forgive me?"

She nodded. "I forgive you, Jack."

He opened the passenger door and helped her inside. "Guess where we're going."

"For a ride?"

"We're going shopping. For food! Any kind of food you like!"

She clapped her hands. "Macaroni and cheese?"

"All the macaroni and cheese you can eat."

But grocery shopping turned out to be more daunting than Marnie had expected. As he led her up one aisle and down another, she clung to his arm, overwhelmed by the choices. When he told her to pick out the cereal she wanted, she stared in astonishment at the towering boxes. She seized one colorful package and tried to read the words. "Corn. . .flakes."

"Just pick one," he said.

She selected another box. "Oat. . .bran. Whole. . .grain."

He seized the box and tossed it into the cart. "At this rate, we'll starve. We'll be shopping until next week!"

Tears welled in her eyes. She hated that tone of voice. "I'm sorry, Jack."

He squeezed her arm. "There's nothing to be sorry about, Marnie. You just can't stand there reading everything on all the boxes. Just pick out what looks good to you and put it in the cart."

That sounded easy enough. She went up the aisle, selected several colorful items, and brought them back to the cart, dropping them in one by one.

He raised an eyebrow. "What did you get?"

She held up a small object.

"Denture cream?" He scanned the other items. "Diapers? Wart remover? Hair dye? Marnie, we don't need any of these things!"

"The boxes are pretty."

He shook his head. "Next time, I'm shopping alone."

She silently trudged behind him for the rest of their shopping trip. She hated the grocery store. It was way too confusing. Too many choices. Too many people. Too much commotion. It made her head hurt.

When they arrived back at the apartment, she insisted on helping with the groceries. At least she would show him she could do something. She wasn't completely helpless. But the paper sack she was carrying ripped open, dumping cans of tomatoes and beans on the kitchen floor. When she stooped down to retrieve them, she dropped them again.

He bent down and gathered up the cans. "It's okay, Marnie. It'll take time for you to regain your strength. You've had a big day. Why don't you go lie down for a while."

"I want to help."

"I know you do. But you don't know where things go."

"Tell me."

He heaved a sigh. "Okay, that bag of rice goes in the lower cupboard. The box of cereal goes on the top shelf. The hamburger goes in the fridge."

She stared at him for a long moment. His words were already scrambled in her head. She couldn't make them fall into place. "Okay, I'll go rest." She went over to the sofa and sat down.

"Do you wanna watch TV?"

She nodded. "I like the show about the judge who tells people what to do."

He continued putting away the groceries. "The remote's right there by the couch."

She picked it up and stared at it. There were a zillion buttons to press. She turned it over in her hand. It looked mysterious and alarming. She set it back down. "I'll just sit here, Jack."

"I'll turn it on, hon." He came over, picked up the remote, and aimed it at the television. "There. You're all set."

"Where's the judge?"

"I think she comes on later. You can watch the news."

"I don't like the news. They talk about bad stuff all the time."

"Hey, I have a great idea. How would you like to see the video of our wedding?" He strode over, removed a videotape from the shelf, and inserted it in the video player. "I don't know why I didn't think of this before." He sat down beside her and pressed the remote. "You're going to like this, Marnie. It was the most beautiful wedding ever."

She fastened her eyes on the screen, her anticipation rising. If Jack said it was beautiful, he must be right. A beach scene flashed on the screen. People were milling around, music was playing, and the sun was setting. The people filed into rows of chairs and sat down. "There's my mom," said Marnie, sitting forward. "And my dad."

"Right!" He clasped her hand. "Look, Marnie. Your folks were right there. Keep watching, babe. You'll see yourself in your wedding dress."

She watched as the bride walked along the beach in time to the music. She looked so graceful and happy. Marnie nodded. "She's beautiful."

"That's you, babe. And me. See? I'm standing there waiting for you with Pastor Maluhia. I couldn't take my eyes off you. That was the best day of my life." He made a coughing sound in his throat and looked away. When he looked back at her, his eyes were glazed with tears. His hand tightened on hers. "Do you remember, Marnie? Do you remember our wedding day?"

She pulled her hand away. He was doing it again—expecting her to recall something that had nothing to do with her. She twisted a strand of her hair. "I like watching your wedding. The bride is pretty."

"That's you, Marnie. *You're* pretty."

"No, *she's* pretty."

"You really don't see any connection between you and the girl on the screen, do you?"

Marnie shook her head. "I'm not that girl. I'm me."

He turned off the television and tossed the remote on the coffee table.

"Is it over, Jack?"

"Yeah, Marnie, it's over." He sat back, closed his eyes, and raked his fingers through his hair. For a long while, neither of them spoke. Marnie stared at the blank television screen, waiting. She curled a strand of hair around her finger, then uncurled it, and then curled it again. Why wasn't Jack saying anything? She was used to taking her cues from him, letting him lead their conversations. Her own thoughts were still too random and higgledy-piggledy. Was that a word? It described how her brain felt much of the time.

At last, he stood up and removed the videotape from the machine, put it back on the shelf, and then looked down at Marnie. "Tomorrow is Sunday. Are you up to going to church?" When she didn't answer right away, he said, "I know it's been a couple of months since you were there. But now that you're out of the hospital, I think it would be good for you to go. It's a little open-air church. Very informal. A great bunch of people. They've been praying for us every day. Many of them took turns sitting by your bedside when you didn't even know they were there. I know they'd love to see you again."

She folded her hands under her chin. "What would I wear?"

"A dress and some flip-flops, I guess. Nothing fancy."

"Will I know anyone?"

"I don't know. But they'll know you. They've been in and out of the hospital visiting you. They all care about you, Marnie. They've been pulling for you. They're thrilled that you're getting better."

She gave him a faint smile. "Okay, Jack. I'll go."

The next morning, from the moment Marnie awoke, she felt a knot of anxiety in the pit of her stomach. Any activity out of the ordinary struck her with fear. She hated being placed in a situation where she didn't know what to do, and that seemed to be happening all the time lately.

Even though he'd made pancakes in the shapes of little animals, she was too nervous to eat much breakfast. She drank her juice, ate the heads and legs off her hotcakes, then pushed the plate away. "I'm done. Let's go."

"But you're not ready yet. You're still in your robe. And your hair's a mess."

"Oh."

He helped her style her hair with the flat iron and rubbed the redness from her cheeks where she had put on too much blush. He tied the ribbon around her mint green cotton dress and made sure her flip-flops matched. He was wearing a green polo shirt and khaki slacks.

"Look, we match," she said as they headed out the door.

On the way to church, she bombarded him with questions. "What will we do in church, Jack?"

"Sing, pray, read the Bible, listen to Pastor Maluhia's message, visit with our friends."

"Do I have friends there, Jack?"

"Of course you do. You just don't remember them."

"Will you stay with me?"

"Right by your side every minute."

"Will I have to talk?"

"Just smile and say hello and let everyone else do the talking."

"Okay. Smile—hello. Smile—hello."

But by the time they pulled into the parking lot, Marnie couldn't remember any advice he had given her. She knew only that she was terrified. Oh, if only she could be back at the hospital—or even at the apartment—where she knew what to expect.

"Where's the church?" she asked as he led her toward a structure with a roof but no sides.

"This is it. Like I said, it's an open-air church. We love to worship in the great outdoors."

She had expected to see a huge church with a steeple and stained glass windows, like the one she had attended in Michigan. This church was more like a garden with lots of trees and greenery surrounding a cozy meeting area.

From the moment they arrived, they were greeted like royalty. "Oh, Marnie and Jeff, how wonderful to see you both again," said a small Asian woman who gripped Marnie's hand and seemed unwilling to let it go.

Marnie smiled. "Hello."

An elderly couple approached and took turns embracing Marnie. They both talked at once with such excitement that she couldn't understand a word they said. She smiled and said, "Hello."

Soon, a group of people had gathered around them, everyone talking and laughing and hugging Marnie.

"*Pehea `oe?* How are you, dear?"

"We've prayed for you at every service, Marnie."

"Aloha, Marnie. It's so good to have you back."

"We sat with you in the hospital. Do you remember, Marnie?"

"Your husband has been a gem. He never left your side."

"We'll be bringing in more meals until you're up to cooking again, Marnie. Let us know what you like."

"I don't know," she murmured. "Maybe macaroni and cheese. And peanut butter and jelly sandwiches."

"Oh, we can do better than that, dear."

"You look like your old self again, Marnie. What a wonderful answer to prayer!"

Marnie's head started spinning. She felt the way she had at the supermarket—dizzy, breathless, overwhelmed. She wanted to run away, but her legs felt wobbly as noodles. She clutched Jeff's arm. He slipped his arm around her, thanked everyone for their loving concern, then led her through rows of white plastic lawn chairs to a seat near the front, where a keyboard, guitars, and a small lectern stood.

Marnie was never so glad to sit down. She was even happier when the service started. That meant no one else would be coming up and hugging her and chattering about things she couldn't comprehend.

While she loved the praise and worship music, her mind wandered during prayer time. And shortly into the pastor's sermon, she found herself fidgeting. She kicked off her flip-flops and tapped her feet against the cold cement floor. As hard as she tried to concentrate on his words, her thoughts kept flitting off to distant places.

"When can we go?" she asked.

He put his finger to his lips. "Soon. Be quiet and listen."

She didn't want to listen. As far as she was concerned, the words were gobbledygook. They were gone long before she could catch their meaning. Why sit and listen to something she didn't understand?

"I want to go home, Jack," she whispered.

He shushed her again.

She crossed her arms, scooted down in her chair, and tapped her fingers on her elbows. Her eyes fixated on a bright green gecko crawling over the lawn chair in front of her. She reached for it, but it jumped to the floor and scurried away. Then she sat back again and started humming.

Jeff scowled at her. "Stop it, Marnie. You're in church!"

"I want to go home."

"It's not time yet."

"Why not? I'm tired."

"Please stop complaining!" He looked around. Marnie followed his gaze. People were watching. Even the minister had paused. There was dead silence. Before Marnie realized what was happening, her angry companion stood up, grabbed her hand, and pulled her to her feet. Without a backward glance, he led her down the aisle and out to the car.

As he opened the door for her, he snapped, "I hope you're happy. That's the last time I'm taking you to church!"

She jutted out her lower lip. "Good! I don't want to come back."

His angry scowl faded. Tears glazed his blue eyes. "Baby, I'm sorry. Of course I'll bring you back to church." He took her in his arms. "You just make me so crazy I say things I don't mean. Forgive me?"

She turned her face away from his. "Just take me home, Jack."

six

Hey, Nate—is that a new shirt?" Shielding his eyes from the sun, Jeff watched his buddy sauntering toward him along Ali'i Drive, a two-lane road that curved around Kona's Kailua Bay. They had agreed to meet at the gift shop beside Hulihe'e Palace, a historic two-story mansion on an expansive, manicured lawn. The palace was next to the seawall, Jeff's favorite spot in Kona.

"So you like my shirt?" Nate asked. The two exchanged friendly cuffs on the arm. "I got it at that little shop on Water-front Row."

"Man, that shirt must have every kind of flower in Hawaii in there somewhere."

Nate flicked his silk collar. He didn't seem to mind that the shirt hung loose on his lanky frame. "Yeah, I thought it was pretty cool. Lots of color, huh?"

Jeff nodded, stifling a grin. "More colors than I knew existed."

"So what's up, bro?"

Jeff shrugged. "Nothing much. I've been walking all morning, trying to clear my head." On a lark, he had phoned Nate and asked him to meet him here, but now, he was having second thoughts. He felt awkward, at a loss for words.

Nate fell into step beside him. They passed a row of banyan trees then the palace and headed for the seawall. "There's gotta be more. What's going on?"

"Nothing," Jeff insisted. Nothing he could put into words anyway.

"You sure? On the phone, you sounded pretty upset."

"I don't know why I called you. It was stupid. You're probably deep into studying for tests or something."

"No more than you."

They ducked under a low-hanging tree, sidestepped the standing puddles of seawater, and hopped up onto the jagged lava rock wall. It was smooth on top, its four-foot-wide surface covered with a layer of cement. Jeff liked walking the seawall; he came here whenever he wanted to get away from his studies and soak up some sun and local culture. He always stopped at the quaint little shop across the street for some Hawaiian "shave ice" with coconut ice cream in the middle. Then he would sit on the wall and ponder the world, watching tourists and sea turtles at the same time.

"So are you gonna tell me what's going on, Jeff, or do I have to drag it out of you?"

"It's nothing, man. Nothing and everything." They walked north, passing several fishermen bent over their poles, until they reached a spot where the waves weren't crashing as hard against the wall. They sat down, facing the ocean. A balmy April breeze ruffled the cerulean waters. Jeff could almost taste the salt spray on his lips. Fleecy cotton-ball clouds dotted the blue sky. It was the kind of day he and Marnie used to love. They had sat here just like this, talking, daydreaming, watching the sunset, planning their future. *What future?* he wondered now. Who knew it would turn out like this?

"Is this about Marnie?" asked Nate, his eyes fixed on the horizon.

"What else?" Jeff kept his gaze straight ahead, too. It was easier not making eye contact. Several outrigger canoes rolled over the waves. The sea was so clear he could spot schools of fish zigzagging through the water and large sea turtles bucking the current.

"Has she had a setback?"

"No, nothing like that." They were talking over the din of roaring breakers, blaring traffic, and laughing children.

"What then?" said Nate. "From what I've seen, she's amazing. She's back in school. Catching up on her classes. Looking and acting like the old Marnie."

"I know. It's going on two months since she came home, and I've never seen anyone work harder than she has. Classes, rehab, counseling, therapy—she's trying to do it all. Of course, the mental stimulation is more important for her recovery than whether she gets the credits. She still has trouble with her short-term memory. She makes lists constantly—everything she does goes on a list. And she can't find her way out of a paper bag. Worst of all, she still doesn't remember me. But otherwise, she's gone from being a helpless, confused child to a practically normal woman again."

"Isn't that what you want?"

"Sure it is." Jeff cracked his knuckles. "But everything's different. Marnie. Me. Our marriage."

Nate gave him a sidelong glance. "You saying your marriage is in trouble?"

"That's just it," said Jeff. "There is no marriage. We're coexisting like strangers forced to share the same living space. Polite but distant. She's wary of me. I don't even think she likes me."

"Come on, man. She loves you. Um, she just doesn't remember you."

"And that's supposed to reassure me? What if she never remembers me?"

"But she's there. Living in your apartment. That has to count for something."

"Truth is, I don't know how long she'll stay. I have a feeling someday I'll come home and she'll be gone."

"Where would she go?"

"I don't know. Michigan maybe. I really think she'd like to go back to the mainland and live with her parents."

"Have you tried talking things out with her? Maybe something will jog her memory."

"I've talked till I'm blue in the face. Nothing gets through to her. I'm telling you, Nate; in our wedding vows we said, 'for better, for worse. . .in sickness and in health.' To me, they were just nice words. I didn't think about what they meant. But they're heavy-duty. There's a whole lot hanging on those words. I don't know if I can live up to them."

Nate swiveled and looked him square in the face. "You thinking of ending your marriage?"

Jeff picked up a chipped piece of concrete and pitched it into the ocean. "I'm saying there is no marriage. Not in Marnie's eyes. It's like I don't even have a wife. These days, it's all in name only. I'm still sleeping on a hard cot in the spare bedroom. How does a guy deal with that?"

"I don't know what to say, buddy."

"The trouble is, there's no chance to work things out. We hardly even see each other anymore. She's always in class or rehab. I'm busy with my classes or putting in additional hours doing carpentry or maintenance work to bring in a little extra cash. Our medical bills are astronomical."

"I thought your car insurance covered the medical expenses."

"It has paid a lot of them, but it doesn't cover everything."

"Sorry, man."

Jeff ran his hand over the wall's smooth surface. "There's something else that gets to me."

"Yeah? What's that?"

"Marnie doesn't like to go to church anymore. She says she doesn't know anyone, and she has no desire to get reacquainted. It drives me up a wall, Nate. She doesn't remember all the people she used to care so much about, even though they're still dropping in and bringing us food now and then. She has no interest in reading the Bible or praying. And when I talk about us going to the mission field someday, she says she doesn't want to go. I'm telling you, man, my whole life's hanging in the balance. Marnie and I were totally committed to becoming missionaries. That's why we're here at University of the Nations. Do I have to give up my dreams because my wife can't remember what God called us to do?"

Nate let out a sigh. "Wow, that is heavy. I don't have any answers for you, Jeff—except for the standard advice you already know. Trust God. Keep praying. Be a good husband even if Marnie doesn't see herself as your wife."

Jeff nodded. "Yeah, I know what you're saying. I was just hoping there might be some easy answers out there."

"None that I know of." Nate leaned back on his hands and gazed up at the sky. "What about Marnie's girlfriends? Has she made any connections with them?"

"You know Marnie. She was friends with just about everyone. When we were dating, she had so many friends I could hardly get her undivided attention. Of course, once we got married, we spent a lot of time together, just the two of us. But she still kept in touch with her friends."

"And now?"

"Now when they drop by, she's polite, but I can tell she doesn't feel any connection with them anymore. When they invite her out, she always says no."

"There was one girl she hung out with a lot," said Nate. "She was in your wedding. What was her name?"

"Jenny. Jenny Purkeypile."

"Is that her last name?"

"Yeah, I think it's German."

"Don't they call her Perky—or something like that?"

"Yep. Perky. The name fits her to a tee. Her family came from Germany, and she's hoping to go back as a missionary someday. She and Marnie were as close as sisters."

"That's good," said Nate. "As I recall, Jenny—or Perky—is pretty upbeat, with a good sense of humor. I think she'd be great for Marnie."

"True." Jeff gazed out at a cruise ship docked in the harbor. Its white hull glistened in the sunlight. He wouldn't mind sailing off somewhere and forgetting his troubles. "The thing is, Jenny's been on a mission trip to Cambodia for the past few months. But I heard she's due back any day now."

"Get in touch with her, bro. I'm sure she'll want to see Marnie. And maybe, she can stir up a few memories."

Jeff nodded. "It's worth a try. Nothing else has worked."

❧

Marnie stood staring into her closet, her latest list in her hand. She was wearing her comfy chemise top and lounge pants, but Jeff would be home soon to take her to her therapy session, so she must select something appropriate to wear. Making decisions was one of the hardest tasks she faced these days. It was easier when Jeff picked something out of her closet and told her to put it on, but he had insisted she start making her own choices. Choosing something to wear was almost as daunting as selecting the right items at the grocery store.

She looked at her list. Yesterday she had worn her skinny jeans and red drawstring top; the day before, her blue-striped tee and tan cargo pants. What should she wear today? She took down her yellow kimono top and khaki skirt. Did they go together? She had no idea.

She laid the outfit on her bed, then she stooped down and foraged among her shoes for a matching pair. More than once, she had left the house with mismatched shoes. She found a pair of canvas wedges, sat down on the bed, and examined them. Yes, they were the same.

So much of her time was spent making lists of things and diagrams of places, and reading material over and over again. Would her mind ever work right? Would she ever feel like a whole person again?

The doorbell rang, so she dropped the shoes and scurried to answer it, hoping it wouldn't be someone she was supposed to know. She opened the door to an attractive woman about her age, with short brown hair and a smile that lit up her round pixie face.

"Marnie, hi!"

The girl grabbed her in a bear hug, but Marnie gently disengaged herself, wondering, *Who on earth is this person?*

"Marnie, it's me. Jenny. Do you remember me?"

Marnie shook her head. "I don't remember anybody. Nobody here in Hawaii anyway."

The girl flashed a sympathetic smile. "I know. Jeff told me."

"He did?"

"Yes. He phoned me. I just got home from Cambodia yesterday. Great timing, huh? I had heard about your accident and was planning to call you. But after Jeff phoned, I decided to come right over. Do you have time to visit?"

"I have a therapy session."

"Maybe I could stay for just a minute."

"I guess so." Marnie reluctantly stepped aside and let her enter. The girl followed her inside and sat down beside her on the wicker sofa.

"How are you feeling, Marnie?"

"Okay. I forget things. Are we friends?"

The girl beamed. "Best friends. I was maid of honor in your wedding."

Marnie twisted a raveling on her chemise top. "I don't remember. I saw the video. It was very pretty."

"You were the most beautiful bride ever. Jeff was the happiest man alive."

"I don't remember him, either."

"I know. But someday you will. He loves you so much. I hope I find a guy like him someday."

Marnie pulled at the ravel. She hated trying to make conversation. There never seemed to be anything to say. She looked up at the girl. "What is your name?"

"Jenny. Jenny Purkeypile."

"That's a funny name."

"I know. Everyone teases me. They call me Perky. But you call me Jenny."

"Jenny. I'll write it on my list." She picked up a small tablet on the coffee table and wrote down the name. "I keep lists of everything, or else I'll forget."

"Good idea. I should try that myself."

"Why? Do you forget?"

"Sometimes. We all do."

"I feel like I'm the only one."

"Well, you're not. And from what Jeff says, you've done a fantastic job with your therapy and getting back into your classes."

"I have to read my assignments over and over again."

"Not many of us would be that diligent," said Jenny.

Marnie smiled. "You're nice. I like you."

Jenny clasped her hand. "I like you, too. We always have a great time together."

"Were you here before?"

"Not since before your accident," said Jenny. "I've been in Cambodia."

"What were you doing there?"

"I was taking care of children who were abused or mistreated."

"That's a nice thing to do."

"I think I was blessed more than the children. They were so eager for love and attention. Families there are so poor, and young girls there are often sold into slavery. It's very sad."

Marnie nodded. She had been on a mission trip, but she couldn't remember where.

Jenny was still flashing her radiant smile. "We held day camps and vacation Bible schools. I had the chance to lead lots of little children to Jesus. It was beautiful to see their faith growing."

Marnie looked down at her hands. "I don't talk to Jesus anymore."

Jenny looked intently at her. "Why not?"

Marnie shrugged. "I don't know."

"He still loves you, Marnie. He wants to be there for you."

"Then why did He let the accident happen?"

"I don't know." Jenny drew in a deep breath. "Some things we'll never understand until we're in heaven with Him. But whatever God does, it's because He loves us."

"That's what Jack—uh, I mean Jeff—says."

"He's right." Jenny stood up. "I guess I'd better go and let you get ready for your therapy session."

Marnie got up and walked her to the door. "Will you come back?"

"I'd love to. Whether you remember me or not, we're still friends."

"Friends," Marnie repeated. "I have your name on my list. I won't forget you."

"I'll never forget you, either." Jenny gave her a quick hug. Marnie didn't pull back this time. Jenny's eyes glistened. "We have a lot to catch up on, my friend. Take care of yourself." She blinked then turned away. "I'll see you soon!"

After watching the slender girl go down the sidewalk to her car, Marnie shut the door and returned to her wicker sofa. She looked at the tablet where she had written in large letters: J-E-N-N-Y. She repeated the name several times.

She was determined to remember this girl with the smiling face the next time they met. It wouldn't be easy. Dr. Forlani had told her she suffered from a condition called "face blindness." Even when she got acquainted with people, she wouldn't necessarily recognize them the next time they met.

"I will remember. I will!" Clutching her pen, she traced Jenny's name over and over, until the letters were thick and black and the pen dug through the paper. "Jenny," she said again, enunciating each syllable. "My friend. . .Jenny."

seven

I have a new friend," Marnie told Jeff when he arrived home to drive her to her therapy session.

"A new friend?" He came inside and gave her a quick kiss on the cheek. "Who is it?"

Marnie retrieved her tablet from the coffee table. "Here. Look. Her name is Jenny."

Jeff smiled. "So she gave you a call, huh? I was hoping she would."

"No. She came over. She sat right here, and we talked. I like her. She's really nice."

"Of course you like her. She's your best friend. She was even in our wedding."

"She told me. I'll look for her when you show me the video again."

"Great. We'll do that. You'll have to invite her back again."

"I'd like that."

Jeff sat down in his black beanbag chair. "Maybe we could have her over for dinner sometime. I'd like to hear how she liked Cambodia."

Holding up the tablet, Marnie carefully ran her finger over Jenny's name. "When can we have her over?"

"Anytime you want. How about tomorrow night?"

Marnie set the tablet aside. "Yes! Tomorrow night! What day is that?"

"Tuesday."

"Do I have classes on Tuesday?"

"Yes. And I work. But we can get home in time for dinner."

"Great! Call Jenny. Tell her to come over tomorrow for dinner."

"Sure. I think I have her number on my cell phone."

"What will we eat?"

"We can order a pizza."

"No pizza, Jack—I mean, Jeff." Marnie walked over to their little kitchenette and browsed through the cupboards. She pulled out a cookbook. "I'm going to cook dinner myself."

He gave her a searching glance. "Are you sure? You're still just finding your way around the kitchen."

"I make macaroni and cheese. I can cook lots of things now."

"Yeah, with a little help from yours truly."

"Call her, Jeff. Call her now."

"Right now, I've got to get you to therapy. I'll call her this evening, okay?"

Marnie jutted out her lower lip. "Okay. I guess I can wait."

But she had a hard time concentrating on her therapy that afternoon. Her mind kept wandering to her new friend and the dinner she would fix. Marnie would show both Jeff and Jenny that she was becoming a capable person again. She could do things on her own. She could cook a simple dinner. She could be like other people who did things without even having to think about them.

That evening, after Jeff confirmed that Jenny would be joining them tomorrow for dinner, Marnie sat down at the kitchen table and thumbed through her cookbook. "What can I fix? It has to be really good."

Jeff sat down, too. "How about spaghetti? That's pretty easy. You can't go wrong with spaghetti."

Marnie nodded. "I like spaghetti. But what about dessert?"

"I can buy something."

"No, I'm making it myself."

"How about cookies in a tube? You always like them."

"Okay. I can do that."

"We'll go shopping tomorrow." He reached for her hand. "We'll get some salad fixings, too. It'll be a great dinner, Marnie."

"You can't help me."

"I won't. It's your party, okay?"

"I love parties."

He grinned. "That's right. You always loved parties."

But Marnie didn't feel quite so confident the next afternoon as she stood in her kitchen trying to decide where to begin. She had insisted that Jeff go run errands and let her work alone. She was so tired of having to depend on other people for help. She needed to do this by herself. How hard could it be—spaghetti, a salad, and cookies?

She got out her cookbook and looked up spaghetti. She must have made it a dozen times, but she had no memory of it. She would follow the recipe step by step. That way she couldn't go wrong. She found the recipe. Okay, so far so good. She looked around the kitchen. She would have to remember where everything was—pans, utensils, spices, pasta, tomato sauce.

She opened the bottom cupboard. Yes, the pans were there. She removed a large kettle for the pasta and another one for the sauce. She would be making a salad, too. She would need lettuce, tomatoes, and dressing. They would all be in the fridge. Yes, they were there. And the cookies. A tube of chocolate chip cookies sat on the shelf above the head of lettuce.

But it was too soon for the lettuce and cookies.

She looked around. She needed to preheat the oven. Okay, that was done. There was the table to set, too. Three place settings. Dishes were on the top shelf on the right. No, those were glasses and mugs. She tried the cupboard on the left. Yes, plates and bowls. She took out three place settings and arranged them on the table. Silverware next. She looked in one drawer then another. The third drawer was the charm. But did the knife go on the left or right? And the fork? Oh well, she would put them all on the plate.

She looked at the clock. Was dinner supposed to be at five or six? When would Jeff be home? When would Jenny arrive? She couldn't remember.

They could be here at any moment! She had better get the

spaghetti started. She took the kettle to the sink, filled it nearly to the brim, and set it on the stove. She turned the burner on high.

Now for the sauce. She read over the recipe again. She needed olive oil, an onion, a clove of garlic, a large can of Italian tomatoes, fresh basil, oregano, ground round steak, and tomato paste. She had forgotten how many ingredients a simple dish like spaghetti required.

She gathered the ingredients from the refrigerator and cupboards and set them on the countertop. She started chopping the onion and garlic then noticed that the water was already boiling. She dropped in the dry pasta, stirred it, then returned to her chopped onion. A whiff of onion juice stung her eyes, sending tears coursing down her cheeks. She grabbed a dish towel and wiped her eyes, but when she looked back at the cookbook, her tears blurred the words. She blinked until the words finally came into focus.

Simmer ground round, onion, and garlic in olive oil in heavy skillet.

She got out a skillet, poured in the olive oil and stirred in the ground round and half-chopped onion and garlic. She was adding the basil and oregano when she noticed the pasta boiling over. With one hand, she tossed the spices into the pan; with the other, she grabbed the knob and turned off the pasta. But it was too late. The white billowing foam had surged over the edge of the kettle, drenching the stovetop and streaming onto the floor.

No, no, no!

She grabbed several paper towels and wiped up the floor. Then she drained the pasta. This wasn't going the way she had planned. Why did so many things have to be done all at once? *Focus, Marnie, focus!*

While the meat simmered, she worked on the sauce, adding tomatoes and seasonings. As she turned on the flame under the sauce, she thought of the cookies. They would take awhile to bake. She got the tube out of the fridge, sliced the dough onto a cookie sheet, and put them in the oven.

Her head was hurting, so she sat down at the table and closed her eyes. *What do I do next?* She looked down at her clothes. She had spilled tomato sauce on her top. She got up and headed for her closet. She would pick something special to put on.

She stood for a long while staring into the closet. Whenever she faced too many choices, her mind shut down. She had to make a decision. Finally, after trying on half a dozen outfits, she reached in and selected a simple green shirtdress. As she slipped it on, she smelled something burning. At the same moment, the smoke alarm broke the silence with its shrill, high-pitched scream. She ran back to the kitchen and grabbed the skillet off the stove. The meat was scorched, but that wasn't what she smelled. The cookies! As she opened the oven, black smoke billowed out. She stepped back and coughed. Her chocolate chip cookies had become little black, smoldering lumps of coal! With a pot holder, she gingerly removed the cookie sheet and dumped it into the sink. So much for dessert!

With the smoke alarm still blasting, she checked the spaghetti sauce. It was bubbling fiercely, so she stirred it and lowered the flame. Then she checked the scorched meat. If she carefully removed the top layer, she could still salvage part of it. First, she had to do something about that deafening alarm. She pulled a chair over, stepped up, and finally found the button that turned it off. Returning to the stove, she picked up the skillet and with a spatula removed all the meat that wasn't burned and dumped it into the sauce. She put the burned meat and cookies down the disposal. Maybe Jeff wouldn't notice there was no dessert.

But what about the pasta? You couldn't have spaghetti without it. She stuck a fork into the white, glistening mound. It was a congealed mass. Maybe a little water and butter would unstick it. After a few minutes, the strands separated. The pasta might be gummy and chewy, but it would have to do.

She tackled the salad next, breaking up the lettuce and slicing the tomatoes. Her head still pounded. Why hadn't she agreed to order in pizza? Because too much was at stake—the chance to feel normal again, to be like other people who took their minds for granted.

She heard a car pull up outside. Jeff! Or maybe it was her new friend, Jenny. She headed for the door. *Please let everything go right. Please don't let me feel like a broken person anymore!*

&

Jeff was just returning home from his errands when he spotted Jenny pulling into the parking area by his apartment. After parking his car, he walked over and greeted her as she was getting out of hers. "Thanks, Jen, for coming. You're a lifesaver. I think you're going to do wonders for Marnie."

Jenny reached into her car and retrieved a brown grocery bag. "I brought her favorite chocolate cake. She's got to remember that."

"She doesn't remember anything that happened in Hawaii. Or anyone."

Jenny looked up at him, concern etched on her face. "I know. It was really spooky coming here yesterday and having her look at me like I was just some door-to-door saleslady or something. I couldn't believe she didn't recognize me. I'm sure glad you gave me the heads-up beforehand."

"Even though she's been talking about nothing else but your visit, she still may not recognize you again. She has this condition called 'face blindness.' The doctor's hoping it will get better as the rest of her brain function improves."

"So she is continually improving?"

"Yeah. She's a hundred percent better now than she was a month ago."

"But she still doesn't remember you're her husband?"

"Oh, she knows it in her head but not in her heart. I'm just the guy who hangs around and makes sure she's on track with her classes and therapy and stuff."

"That must be awfully hard for you."

"Tell me about it. I'm virtually a bachelor these days, with a slightly wacky roommate. Whoops, I didn't mean to say that."

"That's okay. I'm sure you need to vent sometime. If there's anything I can do to help, let me know."

"You're doing it. I haven't seen Marnie this excited since the accident. Somewhere in that foggy mind of hers, she senses how important you are to her. I just wish she felt the same way about me."

Jenny took his arm as they walked toward the apartment. "She does, Jeff. You have to believe that. Someday, the old Marnie will come back to you."

"The old Marnie doesn't exist anymore, Jen, and the sooner I learn to live with it, the better."

Jen smiled up at him. "Well, I'm just starting to get acquainted with the new Marnie. This should be an interesting evening."

"You can say that again. Marnie insisted on fixing dinner all on her own. Usually, I'm there to make sure she gets it right, so this is her first solo. I have no idea what to expect."

"Well, maybe we can both help her pull it together."

Jeff chuckled. "No matter what happens, just keep smiling."

"Will do."

He opened the door and stepped aside, letting Jen enter first. Marnie was right there by the door, smiling expectantly. Even though she looked tired, there was something cute and vulnerable in her face that wrenched his heart. Her long, auburn brown hair was a little mussed, but he hadn't seen her look this happy in months.

"Hello, Jenny." Marnie crossed her arms, as if not sure what to do next.

"Hi, Marnie." Jenny gave her a hug. "I like your dress."

"It was in my closet. I couldn't decide what to wear, so I just reached in and picked this."

"You look great, hon." Jeff was about to kiss her cheek when he noticed a smoky haze filling the house. He wrinkled his nose at the acrid smell. *Great! I knew I shouldn't have left her alone.* "What's burning, Marnie?"

She gave him a frown. "Nothing. Everything's okay, Jeff."

"Is it the spaghetti?" He strode over to the stove. "It smells like you burned it."

Marnie ignored him. "Do you like spaghetti, Jenny?"

"I love spaghetti."

Jeff's voice rose in intensity. "The smoke is thick enough in here to cut. What burned, Marnie?"

She looked at him in exasperation. "It was the cookies. They didn't make it."

"That's okay." Jenny held up her grocery sack. "I brought dessert. Your favorite chocolate cake."

Marnie took the bag over to the counter. "Look, Jeff. Chocolate cake."

"Yeah, that's great." He was having a hard time handling his irritation. Why couldn't he be married to a normal girl like Jenny? Guilt punched him like a blow to the stomach. Marnie couldn't help how she was. If he were the right kind of husband, he wouldn't let things like this bother him. He turned on the fan over the range then went around and opened the windows.

"I'm sorry about the cookies." Marnie's voice sounded like a little girl's.

He took a deep breath. He was being a jerk, and here he had such high hopes for tonight. "It's okay. Don't worry about it."

"Can I help you with anything, Marnie?" asked Jenny.

"Everything's done. I did it all myself."

"I see that. I'd be glad to help you put the food on."

They held hands around the table as Jeff said grace. He was pleasantly surprised that the spaghetti tasted better than he had anticipated.

"Good dinner, Marnie." He squeezed her hand. "You did a good job."

She beamed. "Thank you, Jeff."

As they ate, Jenny talked about her experiences in Cambodia. "I loved going to the little villages and helping with the children. There's such poverty there, and the children are so grateful for such little acts of kindness. Braiding their hair. Telling them a story. Teaching them a song. I loved seeing their faces when they came to know Jesus. Their eyes lit up, and they looked so happy. It made me know I was doing exactly what God had called me to do."

Jeff nodded. "Marnie and I felt the same way when we were in Cambodia. We worked in a teen center in Battambang."

"That's right," said Jenny. "I remember."

"I don't," said Marnie, lowering her gaze. "I don't remember it at all."

Jenny squeezed her hand. "That doesn't change the fact that you helped a lot of people over there, Marnie. God used you in a wonderful way."

"I can't wait to go again," said Jeff. "Whether it's Cambodia or Nigeria or someplace else. I can't wait to be in full-time ministry." He stole a glance at Marnie. She was twirling pasta on her fork. Did she have the slightest interest in what he and Jenny were saying? His enthusiasm waned. There was no use pretending that everything was normal. Marnie had no memory of the most important events of their lives. How could they build a future together if she couldn't remember the past?

eight

Jeff heard birds chirping outside his window long before his alarm went off. Without opening his eyes, he could see the brightness of the June sun against his lids and feel its heat on his skin. It promised to be a beautiful day, but it wasn't starting out that way for him. He rolled over, kicked off his covers, and groaned. This hard cot was giving him aches and pains in muscles he didn't even know he had. He dragged himself out of bed, stretched, and rolled his shoulders. These days, he was going around with a permanent crick in his back.

He headed for the bathroom, but since Marnie was already there showering, he made his way to the kitchen instead and put on the coffee. He was setting the table when she came out in her terry robe, her hair wrapped in a towel. She looked cute as a button. In the old days, they would have had a fun little skirmish with the towel and ended up back in the bedroom. But no more.

"Your turn," she said.

"Do you want oatmeal or eggs? Or both?"

"Both. But you go take your shower. I'll fix them after I get dressed."

"Sounds good to me." As he passed her, he flicked the towel. "You look cute, babe."

She laughed. "Right. No makeup. My hair in a turban. If this is cute, you need glasses."

"So I like the natural look." He took a step then winced and drew in a sharp breath.

Marnie's brow furrowed. "Are you okay?"

He reached back and rubbed the small of his back. "Yeah, it's just that cot. It's killing my back. I don't know how much longer I can take it." He wasn't talking just about the cot now, but that was another story.

She gave him a sympathetic smile. "I'm sorry, Jeff. I know you miss your comfortable bed."

He tried for a solemn martyr's tone. "Yes, I do. More than I can say."

She looked thoughtful. "Well, maybe we can fix that."

Was it possible? Was she saying what he hoped and prayed she was saying? His voice rose on a wave of excitement. "Marnie, you mean it? I can come back to our bed?"

She slapped his arm. "No, silly. I'll switch places with you. I'll take the cot from now on."

He continued on to the bathroom, grumbling, "That's not what I had in mind."

At breakfast, the subject of their sleeping arrangements still played in his thoughts. For months, he had avoided discussing their relationship. Marnie had been too sick, confused, and overwhelmed to make decisions about their marriage. But now, she was almost like her old self again. Even since April, her memory was better; her confidence was growing. More and more, she seemed like the Marnie he remembered. And he was tired of treating her like a sister.

But how to find the words to plead his case? He poked mindlessly at his scrambled eggs. Might as well just jump in. "Marnie, we gotta talk."

"About what?"

"Us."

"Oh."

"I think I've been more than patient, sweetheart. I don't know any guy who would go five months living in the same house with his wife and not expect her to be, you know, his wife! How long do you think we can keep up this 'look, but don't touch' policy? I love you, babe. And I need you more than I can say."

Marnie continued eating her oatmeal, her eyes downcast.

"Are you listening, hon? Am I getting through to you?"

"I hear you," she murmured. "I know it's not fair to you, but I just can't think of you like that, Jeff."

"Like what? Your husband? That's what I am."

"I know. And you have every right to expect your wife to be. . .a wife. But I don't feel it inside. I can't imagine us being more than. . .friends."

Jeff raked his fingers through his hair. This was the last thing he wanted to hear. The old "just friends" rejection. Especially coming from his wife, whom he had promised to love and cherish for the rest of his life. "So what do we do, Marnie, if all you want to be is friends? You want to spend a lifetime together just being friends?"

She looked up at him, her eyes wide and solemn. "No, Jeff. I've been thinking a lot about us. And I've made a decision."

"You have?" That sounded like progress. Usually, Marnie couldn't even decide between brown sugar or maple syrup on her oatmeal. "So what's your decision, hon?"

"I'm going home to Michigan."

His heart skipped a beat. "Michigan? You gotta be kidding."

"No, I'm serious. Our classes will be finished in about a month. It would be the perfect time."

"Perfect for who?"

"Okay, so nothing's perfect about our situation, Jeff. So we have to come up with something that's at least fair."

Anger and indignation were getting the best of him. "You're gonna decide what's fair for us? This I've gotta hear."

Several emotions played out on her face—distress, concern, determination, gratitude. But not love. How he missed that look of adoration he used to see in her eyes. "You've been wonderful, Jeff. Since the accident, you've taken such good care of me. I appreciate everything you've done. But even you have to agree we can't keep living in limbo like this."

Now she was using his own argument against him! "But I never meant that you should go home to your parents. Are you talking about a short visit? Maybe we could both go. I know they must be dying to see you again."

She raised her chin resolutely. "No, not a short visit. I plan to stay."

He was coming unglued. He had to hold it together, or she'd tune him out for sure. "But what about our marriage, babe? We have a serious commitment here."

She hesitated, as if weighing what to say next. "I'm sorry, Jeff. I don't feel married. I have no memories of ever being married. We may have a piece of paper that says we're married, but I can't be intimate with someone I have no memories of. It would go against everything I feel inside. It would feel *wrong*. I know you—we—don't believe in divorce, but maybe we should consider getting, uh, an annulment."

Jeff sat back and inhaled sharply. No matter how deeply he breathed, he couldn't get enough air to deal with Marnie's crazy talk. "You gotta be kidding me! After all these months, now that you're well again, you wanna get an annulment and just take off and go traipsing back to your parents? Give me a break!"

Her lower lip jutted out. "Now you're getting mad. I knew I shouldn't have said anything."

Jeff got up and paced the floor. He picked up a newspaper, rolled it, and swatted his palm. What he really felt like doing right now was putting his fist through the wall. "I can't believe we're having this discussion! All this time, I figured, okay, give her some space. Let her get well. Then she'll come back to me, and things will be like they used to be. But you're not even willing to try, are you, Marnie? You don't have the slightest desire to fight for this marriage!"

She looked up at him with the saddest eyes he had ever seen.

"Don't you see, Jeff? Our history started the day I woke up at the hospital. As far as I'm concerned, there is no marriage. I don't know how many ways I can say it. I don't feel that way about you—the way a wife should feel about her husband. I wish I did. It would make everything so much easier. I see you as a devoted, trustworthy friend. That's all. I can't imagine us ever being anything else. I'm sorry."

All his anger dissolved in those big, sad, earnest eyes. He went to her, pulled her up into his arms, and held on for dear life. Burying his face in her long, silky hair, he broke into sobs—big, racking sobs that shocked him. What kind of man was he, weeping like a child? He felt Marnie's body shudder and realized she was weeping, too. Was this a watershed moment for them—a beginning, a new direction? More likely, an ending. They stood like that, crying like babies, until neither had any more tears.

Finally, he let her go. His emotions were spent. He felt weak in the knees. They sat back down at the table. He heaved a sigh. His mouth tasted dark, bitter all the way to his throat. "Okay, Marnie, you win. Go call your mom. Tell her you wanna go home. We'll do whatever you say."

"I didn't mean I was going to call her right this minute."

"You might as well just go call her and get it over with."

Wiping away her tears, she went and got her cell phone and started punching in the numbers. "Jeff, is it 3541 or 5341?"

"The number's stored in your phone."

"I can't remember how to find it."

He took the phone and found the number for her.

"Thanks." She took the phone and sat down on the sofa.

He sat down beside her, his head in his hands. *Lord, please don't let her go. I can't bear to lose her. You brought her back from the edge of death. Are You going to take her from me now?*

Marnie's voice sliced into his prayers. "Hi, Mom? It's me. . . . No, nothing's wrong. I'm doing fine. My classes are coming easier. My memory's a lot better. And I only need to read things twice instead of three or four times. . . . Yes, Jeff's doing fine, too." She looked over at him. "My mom says hi."

"Tell her I said hi."

"Mom, Jeff says hi. . . . Yeah, we're doing okay. That's what I want to talk to you about. Not about us exactly, but about me. I want to come home, Mom. . . . No, it would be for more than just a visit." Her voice filled with emotion. "I want to come home to stay—permanently. . . . Yes, I've thought a lot about it. . . . No, Jeff doesn't agree, but it's my decision, Mom."

For several minutes, Marnie was silent, listening. Jeff could tell, whatever her mother was saying, Marnie wasn't happy about it. She started twisting a strand of hair around her finger. She twisted it, let it go, then twisted it again.

"Mom, that's not fair. I tried it your way. I've been here for months. It's not going to work. It's not fair to Jeff or me to prolong the agony."

He stared at her. *Is that what it's been for you, Marnie—agony staying here with me?*

She looked at him, as if realizing what she had said. "I don't mean agony. It's just not fair—I can't be his wife—I can't change how I feel. Yes, Mom, I'm listening. I know you have my best interests at heart. Yes, Mom, I know you love me. Okay, if that's how it has to be, I'll give it a few more weeks. But then, I'm coming home, okay?" She handed the phone to Jeff. "She wants to talk to you."

Jeff took the phone. "Hello, Barbara."

A mature, melodic voice replied with a note of sympathy, "Hello, Jeff. I'm sorry Marnie's insisting on coming home."

"Me, too."

"She still has no memory of your life together?"

"We're not even a blip on the radar screen."

"Well, I bought you a little time. Marnie's not coming home yet."

Jeff propped his feet up on the coffee table. "Thanks, Barbara. But I think it's just a matter of time before she's outta here."

"Please don't give up on her, Jeff. She needs you, even if she doesn't realize it."

"It's not me who's giving up, Barbara. Your daughter just

doesn't want to be married to me."

Marnie elbowed him. "Don't blame it all on me."

"Who then?" he shot back. "This definitely isn't my idea."

She stood up and put her hands on her hips. "I'm not going to sit here and listen to you bad-mouth me to my mother."

"I'm not bad-mouthing you, babe!" As Marnie stalked off to the bedroom, Jeff turned his attention back to the phone. "Barbara, you still there?"

"I'm here, Jeff. I have some advice. Can Marnie hear me?"

"No, it's just me now."

"Okay, I have an idea."

"I'm listening."

"I think you should start courting your wife all over again."

"Courting her? You mean, dating? Stuff like that?"

"Exactly. Treat her as if the two of you had just met."

Jeff shrugged. "That's kind of hard to do when we're living under the same roof."

"Then move out. You know that old saying 'Familiarity breeds contempt.' Give her some space. Be a mysterious, romantic suitor. Send her flowers. Bring her candy. Write her little love notes. Sweep her off her feet. She fell in love with you once. Make her fall in love with you all over again."

Jeff scratched his head. "Wow, I never thought of that. I was so busy trying to make her remember the past. You're saying I should start over and build brand-new memories?"

"That's what I'm saying, Jeff. I don't know if it'll work, but it's worth a try."

Jeff was already warming to the idea. Why hadn't he thought of it himself? He swung his feet off the coffee table and stood up. "Barbara, you're an angel! I gotta go make some phone calls and put this plan into action!"

He spent the next ten minutes on the phone. Then, he went to the bedroom and knocked on the door. Marnie appeared, looking red eyed. "Are you through ragging on me to my mother?" she asked in a small, wounded voice.

"I wasn't ragging on you." He went to the closet and pulled down a large suitcase.

She stepped back, her arms folded on her chest. "What are you doing?"

He opened the suitcase on the bed. "Packing."

"Are we going somewhere?"

He emptied a dresser drawer into the case. "Not us. Me."

"Where are you going?"

He dumped another drawer into the bag. "I'm moving in with Nate."

"Nate?" She started straightening the pile of socks, underwear, and shirts. "You're going to live in campus housing with Nate?"

"Why not? He and his roomie have a spare bed."

"I never said you had to leave. I said *I* wanted to go."

"I know. But your mom says you can't go home yet. So I'm leaving."

"Are you mad at me?" she asked warily. "I didn't mean our life is agony. It just came out like that. You know I still have trouble saying the right word."

Facing her, he placed his hands squarely on her shoulders and looked deep into her eyes. What he saw broke his heart. His beautiful Marnie looked so sad, so fragile, so utterly appealing. He desperately wanted to take her in his arms and kiss her until all their problems faded away. But he quelled the impulse. It would only make matters worse.

"It has to be this way, Marnie," he said, returning to his packing. "Like you said, we can't live in limbo. What we had in the past is gone. It's time we both got on with our lives."

She looked flustered, dismayed. "But earlier you said—"

"It doesn't matter what I said. I've come to my senses. For the first time in a long time, I see how things really are." He took a duffel bag from the closet and stuffed in his shoes and jeans. "I'll be around if you need me. I'll still take you to therapy and stuff like that. You can reach me at Nate's place."

"Write down the number for me."

"I will." He carried his luggage out to the front door. "I'll be back tomorrow to pick up the rest of my things." He scrawled several numbers on a sheet of paper and put it on the refrigerator. "If you need anything, here's my cell phone and Nate's and Jenny's."

"Okay. Thanks." She was still hugging her arms, looking bewildered.

He gave her a quick embrace and kissed her cheek. This was tearing him up inside, but it had to be done. "Bye, Marnie. Take care of yourself, okay?"

As he walked out the door, he memorized his last glimpse of her—a wide-eyed, sad-faced girl standing alone in the doorway, a lost soul trying to find her way home. Someday—if he had anything to say about it—she would be the love of his life again.

nine

Marnie awoke and sat up in bed, listening. She hugged her arms and inhaled slowly then exhaled. There was no sound except for the clock ticking and birds twittering outside the window. The rooms of her apartment were eerily silent, as if the silence itself possessed a sound, a reality. It was the sound of aloneness.

When Jeff was here, there was always noise—the shower running, a door banging, dishes rattling, the news channel blaring on television. And there were good smells, too—coffee perking, bacon frying, his aftershave wafting from the bathroom.

Marnie climbed out of bed, pulled on her terry robe, padded to the kitchen, and put on the coffee. She looked around, half expecting to see Jeff sitting at the table reading his Bible. It had been only three days since he moved out, and already, the apartment seemed empty without him. *It has to be this way,* she told herself. *It's not fair of me to expect him to stay here and be my friend when he wants so much more—more than I can give. I have to let him go. And as soon as I finish my classes, I'll go home to Michigan and put this whole painful chapter of my life behind me.*

She poured herself a bowl of cereal. If Jeff were there, they'd be fixing scrambled eggs and French toast together or pancakes shaped like little animals. Jeff made them that way all the time now, just to please her. She hated cold, soggy cereal, but it made no sense to fix a hot breakfast just for herself.

As she ate, she opened her Bible and scanned a few verses. It was what she and Jeff had done every morning after breakfast, and it seemed only natural to continue the routine. After reading the scriptures, they would hold hands across the table and pray, with Jeff doing most of the praying. She was always content to listen. She loved the sound of Jeff's voice when he was talking to God.

"Lord, are You there?" she said aloud. Her words sounded stark and jarring in the empty room. "Jeff's gone. Father, are You gone, too?"

The silence taunted her.

She read several verses in Matthew 10 about God watching over the fallen sparrows. *That means He's watching over those little birds singing outside my window.* They sounded happy, unconcerned about the future. She wished she could be so trusting. She was like a fallen sparrow—wounded, broken, afraid to fly again. If only she could remember what it felt like to sense God's presence, to converse with Him like an old friend. She knew He was real. He had watched over her and brought her back from the brink of death. But He still seemed like a distant acquaintance—someone she wanted to know better but had no idea how to begin.

As she read, her gaze lingered on the words, *"And even the very hairs of your head are all numbered."* What a curious fact. What did it mean? Why would Jesus make such an unusual statement?

Does God really keep track of how many hairs I have on my head? What difference does it make? No one cares about something like that—unless they're losing their hair! But God cares. He counts every hair. A startling realization came to her. *If God keeps track of something that trivial, then He must care about even the tiniest detail of my life—things I would never expect the God of the universe to be interested in. Amazing! He loves me that much!*

She read further. "So don't be afraid; you are worth more than many sparrows." She smiled. The room no longer felt quite so empty. Sunlight poured in the windows where, on the sills, chirping birds sang of God's caring compassion. "You are here, aren't You, heavenly Father?" she whispered. "Help me to feel Your closeness again."

She continued reading for another twenty minutes, until a knock on the door caught her attention. She jumped up from the table, her heart pounding. Who could it be? She wasn't expecting anyone. Or was she? She went to the refrigerator and quickly scanned her latest list. "Nine o'clock Jenny coming to visit."

Another knock sounded. Marnie scurried across the room and threw open the door. Her best friend stood there smiling back at her. Marnie grabbed her hand and pulled her inside. "Oh, Jenny, I'm sorry. Come in. I forgot you were coming. I'm not even dressed yet."

"No problem." Jenny crossed the room and sat down on the sofa. "We're just going to have an old-fashioned gabfest. If I'd brought my robe, it would be like one of our famous sleepovers."

Marnie sat down in Jeff's favorite beanbag chair. "I don't remember our slumber parties."

"One of these days when we have lots of time, I'll fill you in on all the details. We had some really crazy, fun times when we lived on campus."

"That's where Jeff is now. He's staying with his friend Nate."

"Yes, I heard. I remember Nate. Great guy. Always wearing the wild aloha shirts."

"That's him."

"So how does Jeff like living back on campus again?"

Marnie shrugged. "I don't know. I haven't heard from him."

Jenny raised one eyebrow. "Really? I figured he'd be here every day taking you to classes or therapy."

"I'm walking to my classes now. It's a good workout for me."

"Right. The campus is just up the hill on the other side of Kuakini Highway. But what about your therapy sessions? I'd be glad to take you if you need me."

"No, Jeff set it up with the people at church. They're taking turns driving me to the hospital. He gave them my schedule. I never know who's coming until they show up."

Jenny eyed her curiously. "So how do you feel about Jeff cutting himself out of your life like this?"

Marnie thought a moment. "I feel—strange. Every day, I wake up and think he should be here. The apartment feels so empty without him. But I can't blame him. He doesn't want to be my friend. He wants to be my husband. But I can't think of being anyone's wife right now. I've got to get my own life back again."

"Does that mean that someday you may want to be his wife again?"

Marnie gazed off into the distance, absently twisting a strand of her hair. "When I was a little girl, I dreamed I'd be madly in love with the man I married. We'd be the perfect couple and live happily ever after."

"You were madly in love with Jeff," said Jenny. "Take my word for it. I was there at your wedding."

"But the person who married Jeff isn't me. Not the me I am now. I can't relate to her. I can't bring her back. I can't make myself feel what she felt."

"Are you saying there's no hope for you and Jeff?"

"I don't know what I'm saying," Marnie admitted. "I'm still trying to figure out who I am and where I fit in these days." She sat forward, her hands pushing against the beanbag. "I forgot to ask. Can I get you something to drink? A soda or something?"

"No thanks. I've got my bottled water in my bag." They were both silent for a moment. Finally, Jenny said, "I don't think any of us realize what you've been through, Marnie—how hard your recovery has been for you. We can't begin to understand it, because we haven't experienced it ourselves."

Tears welled in Marnie's eyes. At last, someone understood.

"Don't cry," said Jenny. "I just want you to know you're not alone."

"But that's how I've felt—how I still feel." Marnie swiped at a tear. "No one knows how hard it's been. I feel like, after the accident, I was a newborn. I had to learn everything all over again—how to walk and talk and think clearly. I had to learn how to do things everybody else takes for granted—how to open a can of soup or write a letter or use a computer. Only I didn't have years to learn, like a baby does. I had to learn it all in weeks and months. I'm still learning. Sometimes, I feel like such an idiot. I keep forgetting the simplest things—words, names, places, appointments, faces. . . . And I don't think I'll ever figure out how to balance my checkbook or drive a car again or use the remote control."

Jenny smiled. "I'm still trying to figure out the remote myself."

"And I still don't remember anything that happened since I came to Hawaii. Sometimes I still feel like that twelve-year-old girl back in Michigan. That's why I want to go home. I remember my parents and my life there. I want so desperately to be in a place where I remember my past."

Jenny nodded. "I can understand that. But what about the future?"

Marnie shifted. Her head was starting to ache, and the beanbag no longer felt comfortable. "What do you mean?"

"I mean, what will you do in Michigan? Will you work or finish your education or what?"

"I haven't thought that far ahead."

"You left Michigan three years ago because you wanted to become a missionary. You felt God had called you here to U of N."

Marnie chewed on her lower lip. Why did everybody keep talking about her becoming a missionary? "That girl died in the accident, Jenny. She's gone."

"I don't think so." Jenny fixed her gaze on Marnie. "I'm still looking at her."

"You see the outside, not the inside."

"I think the old Marnie is still inside; just give her a chance to find her way back to the surface."

Marnie pushed herself out of the beanbag and went over and sat down on the wicker sofa beside Jenny. "But what if you're wrong?" she asked, searching Jenny's eyes for answers. "What if this is all I'll ever be—a person without a past, a person too broken to have a real future?" A sob tore at her throat. "Jeff is always telling me what a passion I had for sharing my faith with others. He says I wanted to devote my entire life to reaching people for Christ. But I feel such a disconnect with that person. Sometimes I even hate her—the old Marnie—because I know I'll never be like her."

Jenny reached over and patted Marnie's shoulder. "You're being too hard on yourself. Don't worry about the person you were; just concentrate on the person you are becoming. All the good things about you are still there."

Marnie smiled grimly. "Jeff would say I think too much about myself. And maybe he's right."

"Why would you say that?"

"Because, since the accident, I've been totally consumed with myself. I can't think of anything or anyone else. My recovery has taken every ounce of strength and concentration I have. And—I don't know—maybe it's made me a selfish person."

"Not selfish. Self-focused maybe. I think it's more a matter of self-preservation."

"Whatever you call it, somehow I need to find out who I am and what I can do with my life. I don't know where to start, Jenny, except to go back to the home and family I remember."

Jenny paused then asked solemnly, "Have you asked God what He wants you to do?"

Marnie lowered her gaze. "I pray sometimes, but I don't feel very close to God. Most of the time, He's like a stranger to me—someone I know about but don't know personally."

"Then it's time to get reacquainted. Do you mind if I pray for you?"

"Right here? Right now?"

"Why not?"

Marnie didn't want to admit how self-conscious she felt as Jenny clasped her hand and began entreating God to restore the life Marnie had had before the accident. "Make it an even better, more glorious life, Lord," Jenny said with an urgency that made Marnie catch her breath a little. "If the old Marnie would have won a thousand souls to Jesus, let the new Marnie win ten thousand. Restore Marnie's passion for lost souls and give her back her love for Jeff, tenfold. Give them a marriage that honors You and a love that reflects Christ's love for us."

Just as Jenny said, "Amen," the doorbell rang. Marnie jumped up and headed for the door. "I hope I didn't forget another appointment."

A deliveryman greeted her with a long box tied with a large white bow. "Mrs. Marnie Jordan?"

"Yes," she said, stifling the impulse to say no.

He handed her the box then thrust a clipboard at her. "Sign here, please."

Without thinking, she signed *Marnie Rockwell*.

"Have a good day, Mrs. Jordan." Tucking the clipboard under his arm, the man pivoted and strode back to his vehicle.

Marnie carried the box inside and set it on the kitchen counter. "I don't know what this is. I don't think I ordered anything."

Jenny joined her at the counter. "It looks like a gift. Open it up."

Marnie removed the lid and gazed down at a dozen red roses nestled in white tissue paper. "Wow! These are the most beautiful roses I've ever seen." Realizing what she had said, she chuckled and added, "At least, as far as I can remember."

"Well, they're certainly the most gorgeous roses I've ever seen," said Jenny. "Is there a card?"

Marnie picked up a small white envelope and opened it. "It says, 'From someone who cares more than you will ever know.'"

"They must be from Jeff," said Jenny.

"Why would he send me flowers?"

"Because he loves you."

"No, I think he's had enough of me. Why else would he move out?"

"I don't know, but who else would send you flowers?"

"I got lots of flowers when I was in the hospital."

"Not like these. These roses speak of love, not sympathy or get-well wishes." Jenny looked around. "Do you have a vase?"

"I don't remember."

"Let's look and see." Opening one cupboard door after another, Jenny finally found a clear glass vase on a top shelf. "Here we go. I'll fill it with water. You put the roses in."

They both worked at arranging the roses just so. "Have you smelled them?" asked Jenny.

Marnie put her face close to the bouquet, closed her eyes, and breathed in deeply. The most heavenly fragrance filled her nostrils. She sighed with pleasure. "I love them. They're like a promise of new life." She carried the vase over to her glass dinette table and set it beside her Bible. "This will be the first thing I see when I come to the kitchen in the morning."

"Those roses are sure to brighten your day," said Jenny. "Wish I had someone who cared about me like that."

"It's not Jeff," said Marnie.

"Are you sure?"

"He's too practical to spend money on flowers. He'd say we should pay a bill or give the money to missions."

Jenny smiled knowingly. "I thought you didn't know Jeff very well."

"I don't. I'm just guessing."

"Well, he might surprise you. He's that kind of guy."

"It doesn't matter who sent the roses. I'm just going to enjoy them."

Marnie's cell phone rang. It sounded muffled, far away. She looked around. "I can never remember where I put that phone."

Jenny traced the sound to a kitchen drawer. "Here it is, by the silverware." She handed the phone to Marnie.

"Hello?"

There was silence then a familiar voice. "Marnie? This is Jeff."

"Hi, Jeff." It seemed longer than three days since she'd heard his voice.

"Did you get my surprise?"

"You mean the roses?"

"Yeah. So you got them?"

"Yes. They're beautiful!"

"I'm glad you like them."

"It's not my birthday. . .is it?"

"No. I just wanted you to know I was thinking about you."

"Why?"

"Just because. Are you busy?"

"Jenny's here. We're talking."

"Good. Are you busy for dinner?"

"No, I'll probably make macaroni and cheese."

"I'd like to take you out, if you're free."

"Out? Where?"

"I don't know. You pick the place. Wherever you want to eat."

"Okay. I'll stay right here and eat macaroni and cheese."

"That's not what I meant, Marnie. Listen, if you're not free for dinner, how about a drive to Hilo tomorrow? We could go see the World Botanical Gardens. You've wanted to see that place again for a long time."

"I have? Okay, I don't have classes or therapy tomorrow. At least, I don't think I do."

"No, you don't, Marnie. I know your schedule. You're free tomorrow."

"Okay. Then I guess I can go."

"Great. I'll pick you up at ten o'clock sharp. Write it on your list, okay?"

"Okay. Bye, Jeff." She hung up the phone, took her list from the refrigerator door, and wrote down *Jeff tomorrow 10:00 a.m.*

Jenny came over and slipped her arm around Marnie's shoulder. "So, my friend, you have a date with Jeff tomorrow?"

"Not a date. He's driving me somewhere. Hilo, he said."

"Sounds like a date," said Jenny with a lilt in her voice. "First, he sends roses; then, he calls and invites you out for a special day together. That definitely sounds like a man in love to me!"

ten

Jeff pulled up beside the apartment at 10:00 a.m. sharp, just as he had promised Marnie. As he climbed out of his car and strode to the door, he felt as skittish as a cat on a high-tension wire. What was wrong with him? This was worse than a first date. Come to think of it, he couldn't remember feeling this nervous on any first date. He was usually Mr. Laid-back—calm, cool, and collected.

But not this morning.

Everything was on the line—the life he had shared with Marnie, their love for each other, their marriage, their future. What if he couldn't win her back? What if this whole dating thing turned out to be a fiasco?

He straightened his shoulders and rang the doorbell. Even in his favorite plaid madras shirt and cargo pants, he still felt like a bumbling kid in mismatched shoes. *Lord, I could use a little help here. Please don't let me mess things up with Marnie. You know how to get through to her. Show me, too. Help me to win back her love.*

He was so lost in thought that he jumped when Marnie opened the door.

"Hi, Jeff," she said with a little half smile. "Come on in."

"Thanks." He went inside and glanced around. The place looked the same, but it felt like he'd been gone nearly forever. "So how are you doing, Marnie?"

"Fine." She tucked her clutch purse under her arm. "I remembered you were coming over. I didn't even have to look at my list."

"That's good." He couldn't help noticing how fantastic she looked in her tank top and skinny jeans, with the little canvas wedges that made her legs look amazing. She must have finally mastered her curling iron, too, because her long, auburn brown hair looked perfect. He debated whether or not to compliment her. Would she think he was being too forward? He decided to chance it. "You look absolutely gorgeous."

Was she blushing?

"So do you," she said in a small, polite voice. "Handsome, I mean."

"Thanks. I guess we're ready to go?"

"Guess so."

He walked her out to the car and opened the door for her. It seemed strange that they were being so formal with each other, but that was the ritual of courtship. He was going to have to learn those rules all over again. Man, how he missed the easy, comfortable camaraderie of marriage.

As he pulled out onto Kuakini Highway, Marnie asked, "Have you named your car yet?"

Jeff gave her a sidelong glance to make sure she was serious. She was. "Um, no, I haven't picked out a name. Any ideas?"

"I'll think about it. What was the name of your other car?"

"Old Reliable."

"That's right. You told me that."

"I didn't expect you to remember it."

"Old Reliable was wrecked in the crash, wasn't he?"

"Yep. Totaled."

"We were on our way to Hilo."

"Do you remember that?"

"No. I just know."

"People have talked about it often enough, marveling that we survived."

"Are we going to Hilo now—to the same place we were going then?"

"That's what I was planning—the Botanical Gardens and Rainbow Falls. It's where we first kissed. I guess it was a stupid idea."

"Not stupid. But can we go somewhere else?"

"You wanna visit some places here in Kona?"

She nodded.

"Whatever you want, Marnie. You say the word."

"Which word?"

"No, that's just an expression. Tell me where you wanna go."

She shrugged. "I can't remember how to get anywhere."

"That's okay. I remember."

"How about Sam?"

"Sam? You wanna go to. . .Sam?"

"No, silly. I'm talking about a name for your car. How about Sam?"

"Sam's okay by me. You like Sam?"

"I love Sam. It's short and easy to say. Samsamsamsam."

Jeff patted the dashboard. "So where are you taking us, Sam, ol' man?"

With a spontaneous little chuckle, Marnie patted the dashboard, too. "Take us on an adventure, Sam, ol' man."

"What would you like to see, Marnie?"

"I guess it doesn't matter. It'll all be new to me."

"You want the beach, shops, food, galleries, museums?"

"What would you like?" asked Marnie. "You've probably already been everywhere."

"Not really." He pulled onto Ali'i Drive, heading toward Kailua Pier. "We both came to Hawaii to attend University of the Nations. We've spent most of our time in class, on campus, in church, or in ministry. We haven't had time or money to do all the touristy things most people do."

"What did we do for fun?" asked Marnie.

Jeff resisted the urge to say, *We had fun just being together. We didn't need anything else in the world but each other.* "When we could grab a few minutes away from our studies, we'd come to the pier and walk on the beach at sunset, or sit in the sun on the seawall talking and watching whales and sea turtles and tourists in their wild aloha shirts. Or we'd grab a latte at the coffee shop, or hang out with friends, or go swimming, or wander around a bookstore."

"What did we talk about when we sat on the seawall?" she asked with a hint of wistfulness.

"Lots of things. Mainly about what we wanted to do with the rest of our lives—our hopes and dreams, the places we wanted to go, the things we wanted to see, the people we hoped to help someday. We talked about how incredible it was that God had brought us from two distant places on the mainland to this little island in the middle of the Pacific Ocean, and how amazing it was that we had found each other." His voice trailed off. He was saying too much, making Marnie feel uncomfortable. *This is supposed to be our first date. Keep things light, man. Keep things light!*

Marnie gazed down at her hands folded tightly in her lap. "I don't remember my hopes and dreams."

Jeff swallowed over a lump in his throat. Giving her a sidelong glance, he said with more bravado than he felt, "That's okay, Marnie. You can create new hopes and dreams."

She looked back at him with pleading eyes. "How?"

The sadness in her voice knocked the wind out of his sails. "I don't know, Marnie. You just can. It'll take time. You'll form new hopes and dreams, or maybe some of the old ones will come back to you."

She was quiet for a moment. Then, almost under her breath, she said, "I can't remember the past, and I'm scared to think of the future."

He looked at her, almost forgetting he was driving. "You're scared? Of what?"

"I don't know." She paused for so long that the silence between them felt heavy. Finally, she said in a soft, breathy voice, "It's like my life is a big picture puzzle. I had one like that when I was a little girl. It had a thousand pieces. I can't remember several years of my life, but I can see that puzzle in my mind. It was the picture of a beautiful garden with every kind of flower you can imagine. I worked on that puzzle for months. I wouldn't let anyone else help me."

"Did you get it together?"

"Yes. And my mom laminated it and framed it and put it on my bedroom wall. I loved that garden."

"That's a great memory, Marnie—a special part of your past."

With an unsettling urgency, she said, "But what if I never get all the pieces of my life back together? What if too many pieces are missing?"

He reached over and squeezed her hand. "You'll find all the pieces, sweetheart, and your life will be so beautiful it'll make the garden in that puzzle look like an old weed patch."

Marnie laughed and sobbed at exactly the same moment. "Oh, Jeff, you watch the road, okay?"

He had the feeling she wanted to say a lot more, or was it just a vain hope that he was getting through to her? They both lapsed into silence. After a while, Marnie put her head back on the seat and started murmuring in a singsong voice, "Sam, Sam, Sam, ol' man, where are we going today?"

"How about Bubba Gump's?" he suggested. "It's right here on Ali'i Drive. It's a fun place, and they have great shrimp and burgers."

Marnie sat forward and clasped her hands. "I like that name. It sounds silly. Hey, I'm Bubba Gump," she said, faking a slow Southern drawl.

"Then that's the place for us." He pulled into a parking lot across the street from the bustling, movie-themed restaurant. "After we eat, if you like, we can head over to the Kona International Market. You used to love that place. You could spend hours looking at the handmade jewelry and woodcarvings and the local arts and crafts. Once you found these wind chimes that looked like little silver doves. You sent them to your mother for Christmas."

"Did she like them?"

"She loved them. You were always great at picking out gifts for people. You always knew just what people liked."

"Not anymore," she said quietly. "I don't even know what I like."

"I know what you like," said Jeff. "Burgers piled high with tomatoes and onions and lots of catsup. You love Bubba's burgers, take my word for it."

He got out of the car, went around, and opened her door. "And you like french fries thin as shoestrings and so hot and crispy they snap when you break them. I know, because I love them like that, too." He took her hand, helped her out of the car, and they crossed the street. "So for now, we won't think about the past or the future. We'll just concentrate on how much of Bubba's great food we can eat right now." As they entered the restaurant, he added, "And if you want to make a contest out of it, I'll show you I can eat more fries than you."

"No way."

"I will, babe. I'm the french fry king of the world. But they gotta be hot. No cold fries for me."

She stifled a giggle as the hostess showed them to a booth.

"What's so funny?" he asked as they sat down.

"Nothing. Everything. You make me laugh."

He grinned. "That's a start, at least."

She studied him from across the table, her expression hard to read. She looked so much like the old Marnie. This could be a routine lunch date with his wife if so much weren't at stake. He leaned forward, his gaze fixed on her. "What are you looking at, babe?"

"I was imagining a crown of french fries on your head."

"You making fun of me?" He reached across the table for her hand. "You don't believe I'm the french fry king?"

"Not for long."

"Okay, that's it. You're on, babe. Prepare to do battle."

As soon as the waitress brought their order, they tackled the brimming basket of fries, but not before Jeff doused them with plenty of catsup. "The main thing is to eat them while they're hot. That takes total concentration. As soon as they're cold, it's all over."

They devoured the fries between bursts of laughter as the catsup smeared over their faces and fingers. Marnie looked totally vulnerable and appealing with catsup on her face. Jeff fed her the last fry, then he leaned over and wiped her chin with his napkin. "A little too much catsup," he murmured, "but I gladly give up my crown to the new french fry queen."

She smiled. "Is that me? I'm the queen?"

"You're the queen, babe. For real."

She touched her head. "Where's my crown?"

"I'll make you one—the next time we have fries."

"That's too late. I want one now."

"Okay." He grabbed a napkin from the dispenser, made a makeshift crown, and placed it on her head. "There. I declare you Queen of the Fries."

She adjusted the fragile tiara. "It's perfect. I'll wear it always."

Jeff chuckled. "You've already embellished it with some tasty red markings."

"I have?" She looked at her hands. They were streaked with catsup.

She quickly licked her fingertips then looked around self-consciously.

He followed her gaze, knowing she was wondering if anyone was watching their silly antics. No one was. He felt his own tension ease as she put her head back and relaxed against the booth. The old chemistry was still there, in spite of everything.

"You're so funny, Jeff," she said, so softly he could hardly hear her. "I like it when you're funny."

"And I love you like this," he replied, struggling to keep his voice steady.

Marnie touched her paper crown again. She looked the happiest he had seen her in a long time. "Tell me what else I like, Jeff."

"What else you like? You mean, besides burgers and fries?"

She nodded. "Yes. What else? I want to know."

He thought a minute. "Okay, it's probably stuff you already know. You like old black-and-white movies. But only the ones with lots of romance, with girls in long dresses and men in tuxedos, and lots of sentimental music. And when they get mushy, you cry."

"I do not."

"Yes, you do."

"Okay, maybe I do. What else?"

"You like country music, but not the twangy, noisy stuff. You like the old ballads. Let's face it, Marnie, you're an old-fashioned romantic."

"I am? Am I really?" She smiled as if she liked the idea.

He traced a water ring on the table. "You're the most romantic girl I ever knew. And the most sentimental. You cry over a sunset, or a lost puppy, or a sad song. You have a heart as big as the ocean. That's why you'll make such a great missionary someday."

She lowered her gaze. "I don't see myself that way."

"That's because you're still discovering who you are. Take my word for it, Marnie. I know the real you. You're one of the most beautiful people I've ever known—both inside and out."

She removed her paper crown. "Maybe it's time to go home."

He reached for the bill. "Sure, if that's what you want."

The drive home was more solemn than Jeff had expected. He sensed that Marnie was mulling over a lot of things she wasn't ready to confide yet—if ever. He had almost convinced himself that everything was on its way back to normal, but he could see that wasn't the case. He and Marnie might share some light, fun moments together, but she still wasn't ready to let him back into her world.

When they reached their apartment, he walked her to the door and kissed her lightly on the cheek. He felt awkward, and he sensed she did, too. "May I see you again?" he asked, even though everything inside him shouted, *She's my wife! I shouldn't even have to ask.*

She opened the door. "Sure. Give me a call."

"I will. Good night, Marnie."

"Good night, Jeff."

He waited until she went inside, then he turned and strode back down the walk to his car. As he drove back to the campus, he noticed his hands were shaking and a painful lump had formed in his throat. It was all he could do to keep from turning around and going back to the apartment and reclaiming his life with the woman he loved.

eleven

Over the next few days, Marnie didn't hear a word from Jeff. Then, just when she was wondering if she should phone to make sure he was okay, she received an orchid lei and a handmade card inviting her to join him on an adventure to the Mauna Kea volcano. She called immediately and told him she would be happy to go. Her eagerness to see him again took her by surprise.

"I'll pick you up on Saturday at two o'clock," he told her. "Wear warm clothes and some good hiking shoes."

She was wearing a long-sleeved, animal print shirt, cargo pants, and her sneakers when she greeted Jeff at the door on Saturday afternoon. He was wearing a crewneck sweatshirt, stonewashed jeans, black tennis shoes, and a hooded windbreaker.

"Ready for an adventure?" he asked with a wink.

She grabbed her sunglasses. "I'm ready if you are."

"Got your digital camera?"

"I don't know. Do I own one?"

"You sure do. It should be on the top shelf of our, uh, your bedroom closet. While you're at it, grab a warm jacket. It'll be cold and maybe rainy on the mountain. To be on the safe side, I've got some snacks and bottled water in the car."

She smiled. "You think of everything."

"I try."

She was back shortly with her coat and camera. "I don't know how to work it."

"Don't worry. I'll show you," he said as they headed to the car.

After a brief drive, he pulled up beside a bakery in Kona's Lanihau Center.

"Hey, I thought we were going to the volcano," she said as

he parked and turned off the ignition. "Or do we need more sugary snacks before we head up the mountain?"

"Surprise, babe. We're letting someone else do the driving. We're taking a sunset stargazing tour. We're meeting the van here."

She eyed him solemnly. "That must be awfully expensive."

"Only an arm and a leg. But I've been saving up for it. And I had a little extra help besides. It's something we've wanted to do since we got married."

"You don't have to do this, Jeff. I don't even recall wanting to see the volcano. I'm happy with just a walk on the beach or a burger at Bubba Gump's."

He laughed. "We're not having a replay of all those catsup-soaked fries we stuffed down our throats at Bubba's. Listen, babe, this is going to be a night you'll remember. And I don't mean that facetiously—about remembering. They say you haven't seen real beauty until you've seen the sunset from the top of Mauna Kea." His voice softened. "Of course, whoever said that hasn't seen *you*."

She looked away. "Don't, Jeff. I don't know what to say when you talk like that."

"That's okay. Forget I said it. Let's go. Looks like our ride is here."

They boarded what Jeff described as a four-wheel drive, turbo-diesel coach that seated thirteen people. Whatever it was, Marnie was glad to get a seat near the front where the huge windows provided a panoramic view.

"*E komo mai*," said the guide, a stout, weathered man with twinkling black eyes. "Welcome to the experience of a lifetime. *Mauna Kea Kuahiwi ku ha'o ika malie*—Mauna Kea is the astonishing mountain that stands in the calm. It rises 13,796 feet above the sea. But if you measure it from its base on the ocean floor, it reaches 32,000 feet. That makes it the tallest mountain in the world. Does anyone know what Mauna Kea means?"

Someone shouted, "White mountain."

"That is correct," said the guide, his eyes crinkling merrily. "Tonight, from its pinnacle, you will see the most dramatic sunset on earth. After dark, you will view the skies through powerful telescopes. Over the next few hours, I will share with you many fascinating facts about Hawaii, its history, and its culture, so please sit back, relax, and enjoy the drive to majestic Mauna Kea."

Marnie did as the guide suggested. She put her head back and breathed deeply. She had told Jeff she didn't care about visiting the volcano, but already, she could feel an excitement building inside her. Obviously, the new Marnie wanted this as much as the old Marnie. Maybe Jeff really did know her better than she knew herself.

No, that's not possible! He doesn't know me that well. I can't even let myself think such a thing. She promptly turned her attention back to the guide.

"How many of you know how Hawaii was formed?" asked the solid, leather-faced man, as the van traveled along Highway 190 north toward Waimea. He answered his own question. "These islands are the tops of gigantic mountains rising from the ocean floor. Heat from deep inside the earth created magma—molten rock—that rose up through the earth's crust and. . ."

Jeff reached over and squeezed her hand. "Having fun?"

She nodded. But she didn't want to give Jeff the idea that having fun in any way changed their relationship. She couldn't let her defenses down. He was just her friend now. Nothing more. No matter what a piece of paper said, surely her marriage could be annulled, and she would soon be free to go home to her parents. That was the plan that kept her secure, on track. No matter how her emotions wavered, she had to remain focused on her plan.

The guide was still speaking in his pleasant, thickly accented voice. "Mauna Kea is an inactive volcano, while neighboring

Mauna Loa is active. The ancient Hawaiians believed the top of Mauna Kea was heaven itself. Legend has it that Poli'ahu, the icy snow goddess of Mauna Kea, often clashes with her rival Pele, the fire goddess of Mauna Loa, who spews her anger in fiery lava eruptions."

Marnie gazed out the window, her mind drifting, random prayers forming. She was just getting used to praying again. Talking to Jesus comforted her like nothing else did. She was still just beginning to get reacquainted with Him, just as she was slowly getting to know herself again. She still had a long way to go on both counts.

Lord, what's wrong with me? she prayed silently. *My emotions are all over the place these days. Like right now, I'm enjoying sitting here with Jeff. I'm actually looking forward to our day together. I even missed him those few days when he didn't call. I like him, Lord. And yet I can't be what he wants me to be. I can't be his wife. Right now, I don't want to be anyone's wife. Dear Lord, my life is in such limbo. Jeff is part of the past—a past I can't even recall. Please don't ask me to pretend to be something I'm not. Please let him let me go. How can I face the future if I'm still tied to the past?*

"You looking at the scenery, Marnie?"

Startled, she glanced over at Jeff and said, "Yes, I guess so." She felt guilty thinking of leaving him when he was gazing at her with such affection and trust.

"We're on Highway 200—Saddle Road—now," he said, leaning against her shoulder to look out the window. "This narrow, winding road cuts across the island between Mauna Loa and Mauna Kea. Better hold on to your hat."

"I don't have a hat."

"I mean, it's going to be a bumpy ride. Keep watching. We'll be going through Parker Ranch, one of the largest cattle ranches in the United States."

Pushing aside her troubled thoughts, Marnie focused on the passing scenery—rolling green hills dotted with farms and ranch houses. "It's beautiful—and so peaceful," she murmured.

"Almost like a painting that goes on and on."

"It is beautiful, but I'm sure the view from Mauna Kea will beat this by a mile."

"Will we see some actual lava flow?" she asked.

"No. Like the guide said, Mauna Kea is inactive. I thought of taking you to the national park near here to see Kilauea. It's the world's most active volcano. But the park's closed for a few days. The sulfur dioxide levels are too high. We'll go there one of these days though, okay?"

She nodded. It would have to be soon. She would be on her way to Michigan in a few weeks.

The guide was still talking. "Over fifteen hundred years ago, the Polynesians came to Hawaii from Tahiti. They gave Hawaii her name. The Hawaiian Islands were unknown to the rest of the world until January 18, 1778, when English explorer Captain James Cook first laid eyes on Oahu and Kauai. He named them the Sandwich Islands after the Earl of Sandwich."

With a little chuckle, Marnie whispered to Jeff, "What kind of sandwich was it—ham? Peanut butter and jelly?"

"My guess is bologna."

They both covered their mouths to stifle their laughter. The guide didn't seem to notice. He was saying, "In 1810, King Kamehameha the Great united the Hawaiian islands into one kingdom. . . ."

Marnie looked back out the window. She still wasn't able to track what people were saying when they were long-winded. By the time she had made sense of the last thing they said, she had forgotten the first thing. She watched as the van passed a military base then entered a lava field. All the greenery gave way to charcoal gray mounds that seemed to go on forever. Finally, they turned onto the Mauna Kea Access Road—a winding, bumpy road up the mountain, where land formations looked like pyramids. As they ascended the mountain, Marnie noticed that the cloud layer was below them.

"Look, Jeff! We're above the clouds. They look like ocean

waves, only they're white."

Jeff moved closer to her and gazed out the window. "Awesome! I haven't seen anything like that since we flew in from our trip to Nigeria last summer."

"Did the clouds look like that then, too?"

"They sure did." His face was so close to hers she could feel his warm breath on her cheek. "You were as excited as a little kid. You kept saying it was like we were in heaven. We imagined ourselves running and jumping on the clouds and doing somersaults."

"I wish I could remember."

"So do I," he said wistfully.

"Ladies and gentlemen," said the guide, "we are approaching the Onizuka Visitor Information Station. We are 9,300 feet above sea level. We will stay here for an hour while you become acclimated to the high altitude. You will be served a hot meal and issued arctic parkas with hoods and thick ski gloves. Then we will proceed up to the summit in time to view the sunset."

A little cheer went up from the passengers around them. Marnie sat forward and clasped her hands. "This is so neat, Jeff. I can't wait to see the sunset."

He squeezed her shoulder. "I'm glad you're having a good time, babe."

As they exited the van, a cold, dry wind hit them full in the face. People bundled in heavy coats and hats milled around with their telescopes, looking for the best place to stargaze.

"Good thing we brought our jackets," said Marnie with a shiver.

Jeff slipped his arm around her as they entered the visitor center. "If the jacket's not enough, I've got my love to keep you warm."

She rolled her eyes and wrinkled her nose.

"Okay, it's a silly old song my grandmother used to sing when I was a kid. It just popped out. I can't believe I even said it."

She patted his arm. "It's okay. I like silly old songs."

"Good. Then maybe I'll sing it to you someday."

She raised her brows. "Do you sing?"

"Yeah, sometimes. I took voice in high school and even sang with a praise band for a while. Haven't you noticed my old guitar in the closet?"

"Yes, but I didn't think anything of it."

"I'll play it for you sometime."

She smiled. "You surprise me, Jeffrey Jordan."

"Just hang out with me long enough, and you'll learn all kinds of things."

They spent a few minutes browsing the visitor center's interactive displays, information panels, and exhibits. In the small bookstore, they thumbed through astronomy texts and slick paperbacks on Hawaiian culture; they bought nutrition bars and cans of soda at the snack counter, passed over the expensive souvenirs, and helped themselves to free brochures on the volcanoes.

When their guide announced that supper was being served, they sat down with their fellow passengers to tasty meals of glazed beef ribs, teriyaki chicken, jasmine rice, and cucumber salad, with fudge brownies for dessert.

"Wow, I was hungry," said Marnie as she finished her last bite of brownie.

"The cold air does that to you," said Jeff. "Come on. Looks like the van is ready to head up the mountain."

Their guide handed them parkas and gloves as they boarded the coach. Jeff helped her with hers and tied the hood under her chin.

"I feel like an Eskimo," she said as she pulled on the heavy gloves.

Jeff nudged her chin. "Cutest Eskimo I ever saw."

They took their original seats. "I'm so padded I can hardly sit down," said Marnie as she lowered herself onto the leather cushion.

"When we're standing on the top of Mauna Kea, you'll be glad you're wearing lots of layers."

Everyone was surprisingly quiet as the van chugged up the steep gravel road. The ride was bumpy, with jarring twists and turns. "See why we're taking the tour van?" Jeff whispered to Marnie. "Ol' Sam could never make this drive."

"I'm not sure *we* can. This road is scary."

"It'll be worth it. You wait and see."

A half hour later, just before they reached the top, the rough gravel road gave way to a smooth paved road. They had climbed four thousand feet.

"The air is thin up here," said the guide, "so we won't be staying long. With 40 percent less oxygen here at the top than at sea level, you may experience a headache or some nausea. You may feel lightheaded, giddy, drowsy, or breathless." He flashed a wry smile. "You may even find yourself using poor judgment. Don't be alarmed. It's not unusual to experience some of those symptoms. Drink plenty of water. We also provide some hot drinks and shortbread cookies. Stay with your group. And enjoy the beautiful sunset."

Someone asked, "Will we be able to enter the observatories up here?"

"No," said the guide. "Here on the mountaintop, you will see the observatories open their domes and swing their telescopes into position. Mauna Kea has eleven telescopes representing thirteen countries watching the heavens. Mauna Kea is an astronomer's dream—some of the clearest skies in the world. Scientists are able to see the faintest galaxies in the observable universe. But modern telescopes are not made for viewing by the human eye. The astronomers, who, by the way, live in a lodge next to the visitor center, make digital images."

"Then, how will we see the stars?" asked Jeff.

"We have our own portable, computerized telescopes. And you'll find additional telescopes on the visitor center lanai. Your eyes work better at a lower altitude. Don't worry. You'll see star clusters, nebulae, planets, galaxies, and supernovas." With a little flourish, he opened the van door. "Ladies and gentlemen, as the sun goes down, the show begins!"

Jeff took Marnie's hand. "I guess it's time to see that sunset."

Marnie drew in a deep breath. Already, she could feel the effects of the high altitude. He held her hand as she stepped out of the van. Wide-eyed, she gazed around at an eerie moonscape—a dark, rolling wasteland dotted with huge, luminous globes like objects from another planet. The observatories could have been glistening white mushrooms sprouting from black mounds of lava rock. It was an ebony desert studded with black rhinestones. The blue sky was rimmed at the horizon by a rosy white ribbon of light. Beyond the barren rocks was a layer of cotton candy clouds that allowed only fleeting glimpses of the ocean below.

Hand in hand, they walked along the rocky terrain. A silence surrounded them, almost of awe. Fellow tourists spoke in respectful whispers.

Ascending a hill, Marnie stretched out her arms and raised her face to the heavens. "We're on top of the world, Jeff."

He pulled her against him. "I'm always on top of the world with you."

They stood watching the clouds take on whimsical shapes as a changing rainbow of vibrant colors splashed across the blue sky—magenta reds mingling with burnished copper, vivid orange, and slashes of brilliant purple. The view took Marnie's breath away. As the molten white sun hugged the horizon, dazzling beams spiked in every direction.

"When Jesus returns, it will be in a sky just like this," whispered Jeff.

"Even so, come, Lord Jesus," she murmured. It was a verse from scripture, but she couldn't remember how she knew it.

She laid her head against his shoulder. Whether it was the altitude or the amazing view, she felt breathless and lightheaded, even a little giddy. She couldn't remember ever feeling happier than she was at this moment. She raised her face to Jeff's. "I feel like laughing."

"Then laugh."

"I'll make too much noise."

"Who cares?"

"Then you've got to laugh with me."

He managed a chuckle.

"You can do better than that."

"So can you."

She laughed nervously. He joined her. The laughter warmed her cold cheeks and brought tears to her eyes. Between laughs she said, "We've got to stop. People are looking at us."

"Let them look."

The more she tried to stop, the harder she laughed. "I can't stop, Jeff."

"I'll help you." He turned her face up to his, his eyes reflecting the colors of the sunset, and brought his lips down firmly on hers.

Her first instinct was to pull away, but something in the kiss struck a response deep inside her. To her astonishment, she found herself returning the kiss, as if it were the most natural thing in the world.

Later, as they shared a telescope at the visitor center and gazed through the black night at a sequined blanket of stars, her thoughts kept going back to that kiss. While Jeff pointed out the rings of Saturn, Orion's Belt, and the Milky Way, she pondered her conflicting emotions. Was it possible she cared more for Jeff than she was willing to admit? Or was it the seductive enchantment of the mountaintop and the lightness of the atmosphere that stole her breath away and left her head reeling?

twelve

Jeff was whistling a happy tune these days. Marnie's mother had given him the best advice in the world: *Date Marnie as if you had just met. Help her fall in love with you all over again.*

It seemed to be working. In the weeks since their amazing date at Mauna Kea, he had finally persuaded her to go with him to the World Botanical Gardens near Hilo, where they once strolled through the rainforest and first kissed beside Rainbow Falls. Although she had no recollection of that earlier date, she let him kiss her again beside the falls. They shared more kisses during evening strolls along the moonlit beach at Kailua Bay, during intimate conversations on the seawall, and following a Polynesian feast at a luau on the historic estate of King Kamehameha.

He even found the courage to write her a sappy little love song and serenade her with his guitar on the beach. They walked on the boardwalk and shared their MP3 player, listening to Nat King Cole, Frank Sinatra, and countless syrupy, sentimental tunes. They had dessert at the Four Seasons Hotel—chocolate soufflés and fruit sorbet served in the rind of the fruit. When he held her hand in church, she no longer pulled away. More and more, she seemed like the old Marnie he knew and loved. Surely, it was only a matter of time before she invited him back into their home and into their bed.

Tonight might be the night. He was taking her on a sunset dinner cruise on a sixty-foot catamaran along the Kohala Coast. It wouldn't be an inexpensive date, especially for a ministry student, but fortunately, his parents and Marnie's had chipped in some cash to help out. At first, he had refused their offers, but when they had assured him they had a stake in the outcome, he had reluctantly accepted their generosity. He had to agree it would take more than burgers at Bubba Gump's to create an aura of romance that would win Marnie's heart.

He was still whistling that afternoon as he left campus and drove to their apartment. He felt hopeful and confident in his favorite blue oxford shirt and dress slacks. The guys in the dorm had teased him about getting all spiffed up and smelling like a perfume factory. He didn't care. He was willing to do whatever it took to become the man of Marnie's dreams again. He had even come prepared with a single long-stemmed red rose and Marnie's favorite chocolates with the caramel centers.

When she greeted him at the door, he had to stop and catch his breath. She looked stunning in a simple black empire dress and platform sandals. Her auburn hair was crimped in little curls around her face, and her big brown eyes made him melt inside. It was all he could do to keep from gathering her into his arms and kissing her.

He forgot about the flower and candy until she held out her hands and asked, "Are those for me?"

"Who else?" He realized instantly that was a dumb thing to say and kicked himself for dropping the ball in the romance department. He should have made some gallant gesture or said something clever like, *Sweets for the sweet* or *A rose by any other name*—or whatever that saying was. No, he was probably better off keeping it short and simple. He was no Romeo or Don Juan. The old Marnie had accepted that about him; he wasn't so sure about the new Marnie.

"Are these the chocolates with the caramel centers?" she asked as they went inside.

"Absolutely. Would you eat any other kind?"

She shrugged. "I don't know. Would I?"

"Not on your life."

"Then I thank you for knowing what I like even when I don't."

He picked up her black silk wrap from the sofa. "Are you ready to go?"

"I think so," she said as he slipped it around her shoulders. "I had a little headache earlier. But it's better now."

"Listen, if you're not feeling well, we don't have to go."

"Are you kidding? A sunset dinner cruise?" She tucked her small clutch bag under her arm. "You're not getting out of it that easily, mister."

He grinned. "Then, let's get going. Sam Ol' Man is waiting to take us to Anaeho'Omalu Bay."

"Where?"

"Don't ask me to say it twice."

"Can you?"

"I can, but it won't sound the same."

"Where is it—this bay we can't pronounce?"

"North of Kona. About a half-hour drive. Maybe an hour considering Ol' Sam's seen better days. We board the catamaran at Waikoloa Beach."

"I can't wait."

"Me neither. Guess we'd better get a move on so we don't miss the boat."

"You smell good," she told him as they walked to the car.

He opened the door for her. "So do you."

She slipped inside. "It's the perfume in the fancy green bottle on the bureau. Did you buy it for me?"

"I gave it to you when we got engaged. How'd you guess?"

"I don't know. I just had a feeling."

As he shut the door and walked around to his side, he started whistling again. It was going to be an awesome night.

The cruise turned out to be everything he had anticipated, except for an unexpected hitch at the beginning. He and Marnie were overdressed. They should have worn casual beach attire. They had to remove their shoes and wade in ankle-deep water to board the sleek vessel. Marnie laughed as he sheepishly pulled off his shoes and socks and rolled up his pant legs.

But spending the evening barefoot wasn't a problem. He and Marnie were having too much fun watching the colorful Tahitian show; gazing at dolphins, manta rays, and tropical fish through glass-bottom wells; and sampling the *ono grinds*—the tasty food. They were served a scrumptious dinner—fresh fish, London broil with shiitake mushroom sauce, smoked-turkey wraps, hand-rolled sushi, and a tropical fruit platter, with cream puffs for dessert.

"If we ate like this every day, we'd both be blimps," she told him.

He licked the last bite of filling from his fingers. "But what a way to go."

Just before sunset, they found a spot by the railing at the front of the vessel. While Hawaiian music played in the background, couples strolled along the deck arm in arm. The sky was aflame with vivid reds and oranges. A gentle breeze ruffled their hair, and salt spray cooled their skin.

Jeff drew Marnie close and whispered, "If God can paint earthly skies like this, imagine what heaven must look like."

"It reminds me of the sunset at Mauna Kea. I'll never forget that night."

He nuzzled her hair. "Me neither."

She rested her head against his chest. "I believe God gives us skies like this as a silent reminder of what He's preparing for us."

"It's like a teaser," Jeff agreed. "A little sample to whet our appetite for more."

Marnie moved her fingers over the shiny mahogany railing. "People go about their business and never think about the beautiful world God paints for them every day—sunrise and sunset, oceans and mountains, flowers and trees. When I woke up from my coma, I saw everything with new eyes. I came out of such a dark place into so much color and light. Every day, I notice things I haven't seen before. I never want to take anything for granted again."

He hugged her close and pressed his chin against the top of her head. "I never want to take *you* for granted, Marnie. Every day, I thank God that He spared your life."

They were both silent as the vibrant clouds gave way to a cloudless, deep blue sky and the blazing sun shrank to a bubble of light on the horizon then disappeared. With darkness came a chill in the air. Marnie stiffened.

"You cold?" asked Jeff.

"No. My headache's back."

"Anything I can do to help?"

"No, it'll go away in time."

He held her at arm's length and searched her face. Shadows kept him from reading her eyes. "How long have you been getting headaches?"

She shrugged. "I don't know. A few days. A week maybe."

"Why didn't you tell me?"

"What could you do—except look worried like you do now?"

"Is it because of your injury? What does the doctor say?"

"He says headaches aren't unusual with a brain injury. Not to mention the hole they drilled in my skull. Just thinking of that gives me a headache. But he says I'm doing great considering all I've been through."

Jeff hugged her again. "I think so, too. More than great. Amazingly great."

"Greatgreatgreat," she repeated. "If you say it enough, it doesn't make sense anymore."

They tried it—*greatgreatgreatgreat*—and dissolved in laughter.

"Oh great! I can't even say that word anymore. Oh, wait, I just did."

"Then just say I'm terrific. Or fantastic. Or marvelous. Or stupendous. Is that a word?"

"I don't know, but you're all of those. And more."

"Look," said Marnie. "We're back already."

Jeff nodded. The catamaran was approaching the pier. Their magical evening was almost over. "It's ending too soon."

"We still have the drive home."

Home. She said the word almost as if she still considered it his home, too.

She wrapped her arm in his. "I have something to show you."

His curiosity was piqued. "What? Something at home?"

"Yes."

"What is it?"

"I found two boxes in the cupboard—one marked CAMBODIA and one marked NIGERIA."

"Oh yes, I remember those."

"They're filled with letters and pictures and e-mails. And cute little souvenirs."

"They're from our mission trips. We took the pictures. The e-mails, letters, and little gifts are from the people we ministered to. We saved everything they sent. We couldn't wait to go back again someday."

"Is that where you want to go—to Cambodia or Nigeria?"

"Maybe. Wherever the Lord leads. Wherever there are hurting people who need to hear about Jesus' love for them."

Marnie lowered her head. "I've been reading the letters and e-mails. I can't read fast yet, so it will take me a long time. But when I read them, I don't want to stop. I want so much to remember those people and the times we spent with them. I search their letters for details to make the experiences come alive for me. I feel so hungry to know more. It's like all those people hold a key to unlock a secret part of me. They're buried somewhere in my heart, and I need to find them again."

Jeff caught his breath. *This is the old Marnie talking—the woman with such amazing love and passion for ministry. She's back! Thank You, Father. Thank You!*

"Listen, sweetheart, I can help you. I can sit down and

read the letters with you and tell you everything I remember about those days. That way, you can make my memories your memories."

She looked up at him. "Do you think it'll work?"

"We can give it a try."

"Okay. When we get home, I'll show you the boxes. We might have time to read a few letters tonight."

"Sounds good to me. As long as you feel like it."

"I do. My headache is better."

"Good. And if it comes back, I'll rub your temples. That's what I used to do when you had a headache or were stressed out."

"I don't remember."

"I know. It doesn't matter."

"You can still rub my temples."

"Great."

She stifled a giggle. "Not that word again!"

He held up his hand. "I promise not to say it again tonight. We'll just talk about our marvelous, fabulous, magnificent days on the mission field."

Jeff was true to his word. He didn't say *that* word, but he kept the drive home filled with conversation about their days in Cambodia and Nigeria. He told her everything that came to mind. He knew the letters and e-mails would prompt more memories. It was only a matter of time before Marnie's yearning for the mission field would be reborn. And if that love returned, why not her love for him as well?

They arrived back at their apartment shortly before nine o'clock. "Do you still want to read a few letters?" she asked as he walked her to the door.

"I'd love to, if it's not too late for you."

"No, it's not too late." She unlocked the door, and they went inside. "Being out on the ocean invigorated me. Believe it or not, I'm even hungry. I didn't think I'd ever want to eat again after that big meal."

He turned on the lights. "I hate to admit it, but I'm hungry, too. We could have our old standby—popcorn and sodas. If you like, I'll pop the corn while you get the letters out."

She kicked off her shoes. "Sounds good to me."

After removing his shoes, Jeff went to the kitchen and found the microwave popcorn in the same cupboard where it had always been. Everything seemed just as he had left it. He was home again, and it felt so good. *Lord, please let me stay. Let me have my life with Marnie back again.*

By the time the popcorn and sodas were ready, Marnie had the boxes of memorabilia open and letters spread out on the kitchen table. He handed her a soda and set the brimming bowl of popcorn on the table. The aroma of freshly popped corn made him feel even more at home.

"Only one thing is missing," said Marnie.

Jeff looked around. "What? Music?" They had always loved having praise music playing in the background.

"No, but that's a good idea." She turned on the stereo then reached for the box of chocolates he had brought. "I love chocolate with my popcorn."

He chuckled. "That's right. You love eating sweet and salty things together."

She sat down and popped a chocolate into her mouth. "You knew that?"

"Sure. You always eat potato chips with your ice cream and chocolate shakes with your fries."

She shook her head. "I didn't even realize that. But you're right. That's what I do. It's scary when somebody else knows you better than you know yourself."

Jeff helped himself to the popcorn. "It doesn't have to be scary. . .when that someone loves you like I do."

Her face blanching, Marnie quickly turned her attention to the letters on the table.

Idiot! Jeff said to himself. *You can't push her. When you come on too strong, she retreats like a startled deer. Just let things happen naturally.* He reached for a stack of photographs. "Look. These are pictures we took in Cambodia. Even though we hung out together after the spilled-salad incident, it was in Cambodia where we first became close friends." He wanted to say, *That's where we fell in love,* but he didn't want to alarm her again.

He handed her a photo. "Here we are at an open-air market. You loved all the beautiful baskets. And look at all the colorful fruits and vegetables and raw fish spread out on the wicker mats." He handed her another picture. "See, here you are buying a basket. Look how busy the marketplace is—all the little shops crammed together, merchants wearing wide-brimmed hats and stooping over their baskets, hundreds of bikes lined up along the road, and people everywhere."

Marnie looked at the pictures. "I see myself there, but I have no memory of it. It's so frustrating."

"Cambodia is where the Killing Fields are," Jeff said solemnly. "In the seventies, the Khmer Rouge killed nearly two million people—over one-fifth of Cambodia's population."

Marnie's eyes welled with tears. "That's so sad. Is that why we went there?"

"We went there because the people are poor and need medicine and education and training. But mostly, we went to tell them about Jesus. We worked at a teen center in Battambang. But we also traveled to nearby villages with a health-care team. They treated sick children and immunized people. Children over there often die of diseases before they're five. We couldn't treat anyone ourselves, but we held the children and played with them. They really loved us."

Marnie studied him for a long moment, her dark eyes shiny with unshed tears. "You really do care about the people over there, don't you?"

He wasn't sure how to respond. "Sure I do. Once you've been there, you never forget what it's like." He stopped abruptly, realizing what he had said—*you never forget.* "You couldn't help forgetting, Marnie. You were injured. Otherwise, you'd still be remembering what it was like over there, too."

She pushed her chair back and stood up. "My headache's back."

He got up and went to her. "Can I help? Should I go? Do you want me to rub your temples?"

She paused a moment then said, "Okay."

He followed her over to the wicker sofa, and they sat down. She put her feet up and lay back against his chest. Gently he stroked her temples. They had sat like this a hundred times before. Marnie felt so warm and good in his arms. Being close like this was as natural to him as breathing. He could almost make himself believe this was like any other night before the accident—the two of them cuddling on the sofa, grateful to be together and so deeply in love. Yes, that's exactly how it was. He had his wife back in his arms again, back where she belonged. Almost dozing now, she looked so trusting and content. He lowered his face to hers and lightly kissed her lips. "I love you, Marnie."

"Me, too," she murmured sleepily.

Joy spiraled through his chest. *She still loves me!* He kissed her again. She didn't resist.

Impulsively he gathered Marnie up in his arms and carried her to their bedroom. He laid her on the bed and smothered her face and neck with kisses. "I need you, Marnie," he whispered. "I need you to be my wife again." He was so caught up in the moment that it shocked him when she gave him a hard shove backward.

"Stop it! Leave me alone!" Sobbing, she scrambled to the far side of the bed and hugged her arms, looking like a frightened kitten.

He stumbled and grabbed the bedpost to keep from falling. In exasperation he uttered, "What's wrong with you, Marnie?"

She was trembling. "I was half asleep. You surprised me."

He raked his fingers through his hair. "When I kissed you today, you kissed me back. You liked it; I know you did. I thought that meant you were ready to be my wife again."

"I can't." She rubbed her mouth with the back of her hand. "I can't be with you like that. I'm not ready. I thought you understood."

He was still white-knuckling the bedpost. "I want to understand, but you keep giving me mixed signals. Which is it, Marnie? Do you want a husband—or a buddy?"

"That's not fair." She pushed her tangled hair back from her face. "You know how it is for me. I don't feel—married."

"But I thought—I thought tonight was different." His heart was pounding like a tom-tom, and the bitter taste of gall seared the back of his throat. "I thought you loved me again."

"I do," she said in a small, sad voice. "But not that way."

Jeff paced the floor, rubbing the back of his neck. He couldn't wrap his mind around what had just happened. Everything had been going so well. Now it was all up in smoke. "I can't do this anymore," he said under his breath.

"Do what?" Her gaze was silently accusing.

He looked her straight in the eyes. "I can't keep playing the devoted suitor, Marnie." He tried to sound forceful and strong, but his voice came out tremulous, uneven. "I can't pretend we're just dating like some single couple. I'm a husband who yearns to hold and caress and cherish his wife."

She bit her lower lip. "I told you I'm not ready. I don't know if I ever will be. Why do you keep pressuring me?"

"I don't know." He heaved a sigh. "I guess because I had this crazy idea that with a little romance I could make you fall in love with me again. Your mom even thought so. I guess we were both wrong."

"My mom put you up to this?" She sat hugging herself, looking like a sad little waif with her smeared makeup and mussed hair. "This was all a crazy scheme you two cooked up?"

"Don't blame her. She was just trying to help."

"I don't need her help," Marnie shot back tearfully. "Or yours, either. Just go! Leave me alone!"

"That's one wish I can grant." He strode to the door, his breath ragged in his throat, his voice raw with emotion. "I'm outta here, Marnie. And don't worry. I won't be back."

thirteen

Marnie's head pulsed with pain. Over and over, the words throbbed in her mind: *What have I done? What have I done?* She lay curled on her bed, hugging her pillow. In the hours since Jeff had walked out promising never to return, the apartment was accusingly silent. Only her own desolate sobs echoed against the bleak walls. She had never felt so alone.

How could things have fallen apart so quickly? She and Jeff had had a wonderful day together. Her feelings for him were stronger than ever. She was beginning to see why she had fallen in love with him in the first place. She was even entertaining the idea that it could happen again.

And then. . .

And then he had demanded more than she could give.

He had taken her by surprise, and instinctively she had resisted.

And now he was gone forever.

She didn't know who to be angrier with—Jeff for spoiling their perfect day with his sudden ardor or herself for over-reacting and driving him away.

Already, she missed him. How could she be so upset with him one moment and so lost without him the next? Was it possible she was in love with him after all? But even if that was so, she couldn't risk another incident like tonight. Her emotions were too fragile, too volatile, too unpredictable. And Jeff—she couldn't bear to see that look of pain and disappointment in his eyes again. He deserved someone who knew how to be a proper wife.

After a while, between sobs, Marnie slipped into a restless slumber. She dreamed of Jeff. He was holding his arms out to her, beckoning her to come to him. Just when she was about to rush into his embrace, he disappeared. She woke up with a start and called his name. No one was there.

She sat up and swung her legs over the bed. She was still wearing her black empire dress. The night air was so warm and humid that the garment clung to her skin. She didn't care. She stared into the shadows and watched the moonlight from the open window cast faint streamers along the floor. She listened to the clock ticking on the nightstand and the shutters rattling in response to a stirring breeze.

She welcomed the breeze. Maybe it would blow away the gloom and lift the heaviness from her heart. With a sigh, she got up, pulled off her dress, and slipped into an old tank top and cotton shorts. It was three o'clock in the morning, but maybe she could still catch a few more hours of sleep.

She lay back down and stared up at the ceiling. She was wide awake now, and her mind was running in every direction at once. How had she come to this precise moment in time? And where did God want her to go from here? She replayed the long months since she had awakened from the coma. She relived the past couple of weeks with Jeff—their dates, the fun they had had. She went back over every detail of the past evening, trying to understand how things had gone so wrong.

She couldn't blame Jeff for wanting his wife back. And yet, in her heart of hearts, she still didn't see him as her husband. Maybe if he had given her more time. But she couldn't fault him for his lack of patience. If anything, he had been more patient than anyone had a right to expect. He had stood by her through all the craziness, the ups and downs, when she was learning to walk and talk again, when she didn't have a clue who he was or, for that matter, who she herself was. He was always there for her.

Until now.

Now he was gone. For good. He had had enough, and she couldn't blame him. Now it was time for her to find her way alone.

"But I'm not alone, am I, Lord?" she said aloud, her voice filling the darkness. "You're still with me, aren't You? I need You so much. You said that You will never leave me nor forsake me. I'm holding You to that, heavenly Father." She brushed away a tear. "Help me to be strong. Help me to make the right choices. Help me to know I'm not alone."

A fresh breeze ruffled the curtains and brought goose bumps to her bare arms. "You are here, aren't You, Father? I can almost feel You wrapping Your arms around me. I love You, Jesus."

She lay back down and fluffed her pillow under her head. She wasn't alone. Jesus was with her, watching over her. No matter what happened tomorrow, He would be with her every step of the way.

It was after nine o'clock when Marnie awoke to bright, golden sunlight streaming in her window. She got up and stretched. Her body ached from lack of sleep, but at least her headache was gone. It was a new day. Maybe Jeff would call. Maybe he would come back. Maybe last night wasn't as bad as she remembered. Surely Jeff wouldn't leave her after all they had been through together. Even the memory of his kisses was sweet now. She did enjoy being close to him. If it hadn't been for her headache and the way he took her by surprise, perhaps the evening would have ended differently.

She went to the kitchen, fixed a bowl of oatmeal, and poured herself a glass of orange juice. As she ate, she opened her laptop and checked her e-mail. Maybe Jeff had sent a note. She sighed in disappointment. The only note was from a lady at church reminding Marnie she would pick her up at two o'clock for her therapy session.

She checked her cell phone to see if she had missed any calls. She hadn't.

Checking her appointment calendar on the fridge, she let out a groan. She was scheduled to give an oral presentation in her ESL class the day after tomorrow. It was her final project. Her grade depended on it. And she wasn't ready. She had spent too much time lately dating—and daydreaming.

If Jeff were here, he would go over her notes and help her organize her material. When it came to her classes, she still had a hard time making her brain work right. And she still felt uneasy about giving a speech in class. She didn't always say what she intended to say. Sometimes, her words got jumbled and her mind went blank.

"No excuses, Marnie." She got out her textbook and notes. "If I start now, maybe I can get a head start on this before my therapy session."

Over the next four hours, she pored over her textbook and took copious notes even though she had a hard time concentrating. Every few minutes, she would glance at her cell phone and wonder when Jeff would call or text message her. She kept checking her e-mails, certain that he would write one of his brief, funny little notes. Several times she got up and looked outside the door in case Jeff had left her a little gift or flower or handwritten note.

There was nothing.

She went to her therapy session feeling discouraged. As much as she appreciated the ladies at church taking turns driving her to the hospital, she missed the days when Jeff had taken her. His caring smile had always prompted her to try harder and go the extra mile, no matter how difficult the task was.

When she got home that afternoon, she returned to her studies. She kept reading the same words over and over, but nothing made sense. After an hour or so, she gave up in frustration. She felt restless, distracted, at her wit's ends.

Finally, she reached for her Bible and let it fall open at random. It opened to 1 Corinthians 13. "The love chapter," she mused. "How ironic is that?" She scanned the verses. " 'Love is patient, love is kind; love. . .rejoices with the truth. It always protects, always trusts, always hopes, always perseveres. Love never fails.'" She brushed at an unwelcome tear. "That's how Jeff has loved me, isn't it, Lord—just the way You told him to?"

She closed the Bible and ran her palm over the leather cover. "And, Father, that's the way You wanted me to love Jeff, too, isn't it? I'm sorry, Lord. I couldn't do it. But it's a strange thing. The closer I feel to You, Jesus, the closer I feel to Jeff. It's as if by loving You more I'm loving him, too. Is this the kind of love that comes only by knowing You?"

She felt as if she were on the verge of comprehending something she hadn't understood before—the connection between loving God and loving others. The realization was only half formed and still too nebulous to grasp fully. But what she did understand was mind-blowing. True love wasn't something she could generate in her own flawed human heart; it was born out of her love and devotion to Christ. The more she loved God and experienced His love for her, the more she could love others—the more she could love Jeff!

Still mulling over the implications of what she had read, she fixed herself a box of macaroni and cheese for dinner. "If only I had someone wiser than I am to help me understand this whole love thing," she murmured as she finished her macaroni. Suddenly, she thought of Jenny. Jenny was wise and had a close walk with God. She would be the perfect one to go to for advice. Marnie hadn't seen her best friend in what seemed like ages, except for a few minutes here and there at school. She had been too busy doing all the touristy things with Jeff.

With eager fingers, she punched in Jenny's number and waited. Her shoulders sagged when she got Jenny's voice mail. "Give me a call when you have a chance, Jen," she said, trying to sound lighthearted. "I miss you."

After dinner, she forced herself to tackle her presentation again. She had only one more day to prepare. Somehow she had to be ready.

About an hour later, a familiar melody rang from her cell phone. She grabbed it and said hello. Surely it would be Jeff. He hadn't called all day.

It was Jenny. She sounded worried. "Marnie, I just got home

from work. I've been wanting to call you all day. I heard about Jeff."

"Jeff?" Now Marnie was confused. Surely he wouldn't tell Jenny about last night. "What about Jeff?" she asked.

"I heard he's leaving the island."

"Leaving?"

"Yes. I ran into his friend Nate—Nate Anderson—and he said Jeff's moving out."

"Moving out?" Marnie's mouth went dry. "Where is he going?"

"Cambodia."

"Cambodia?"

"That's what Nate said."

"How could he be going to Cambodia?"

"On a mission trip. You mean you didn't know?"

"No. I mean, he didn't mention it—yet. When is he going?"

"I heard he leaves tomorrow. I thought for sure he would have told you."

Marnie swallowed over a lump in her throat. "How could this happen so suddenly? It takes weeks to plan a mission trip."

"Usually, it does," Jenny agreed. "But Nate said someone on the outreach team got sick. Jeff is taking his place. The plane leaves tomorrow. I guess it all just fell into place all of a sudden."

Marnie's head spun. How could Jeff do this to her—leave without so much as a word? Did he hate her that much?

"Jeff didn't tell you he was going?" Jenny asked with a hint of concern.

"No, he didn't."

"Well, it all happened so quickly; he must be frantic trying to finish up his classes and get ready. But I'm sure he'll call you."

Marnie tried to hold back the emotional fireworks exploding inside her. "I, uh, I probably just missed his call. I'm sure that's it."

"Are you okay?" asked Jenny. "If you need anything, Marnie, you'll let me know, won't you?"

"Sure. I'm fine." She realized she was writing Jeff's name over and over in the margins of her presentation. "I'm just busy studying."

"Aren't we all? I'm so glad classes end this week."

"Me, too."

"Maybe we can get together when all the pressure's off."

"I'd like that," said Marnie. "But I'll probably be flying home to Michigan next week."

"That soon?"

"As soon as I can get a flight."

"But you are coming back to U of N for the fall quarter, aren't you?"

Marnie paused a long moment, trying to regain her composure. "I—I don't think so, Jen. There are too many sad memories here."

"I understand," said Jenny with a catch in her voice. "You've been through so much this year. I can't blame you for wanting to go home. But I'll miss you like crazy."

Marnie swallowed a sob. "I'll miss you, too, Jen."

"We'll definitely get together before you go. I'll get some of our friends together, and we'll have a girls' night out."

"Great, Jen. That's just—great." *Great* was *their* word—hers and Jeff's—their funny, happy word.

"Talk to you later, Marnie."

"Right, Jen. Have a great night." Marnie snapped her cell phone shut and dropped it on the table then sat back and closed her eyes. She had never felt more abandoned and betrayed. Just when she was beginning to think they had a chance, Jeff had given up on her once and for all. There was no going back and redoing the past. It was finished. Over. The truth was as searing and explosive as an autumn bonfire devouring dead, dry leaves on a windy night. As a girl in Michigan, she had once burned her arm standing too close to the crackling flames. But that pain was nothing compared to the pain she was feeling now.

Tears rolled down her cheeks and into her mouth; they tasted warm and salty. She sat for a long while, letting the tears flow. It was strange how you could feel so miserable, and yet, it felt so good to cry. Then she got the hiccups, which interrupted the rhythm of her weeping, so she dried her tears and concentrated on getting rid of the hiccups. She held her breath, and just when she thought it had worked, she hiccupped again, more noisily than before. They were getting worse—not better. She tried drinking a full glass of water, but that sent her running to the bathroom.

Then—you might know it—her cell phone rang. By the time she got back to the kitchen, it had stopping ringing. But there was a message. It was Jeff. Her heart thundered in her chest so loudly she could hardly hear what he was saying.

"Marnie, it's me. I'm on my way over. I've got something to tell you. See you in a few."

fourteen

Marnie ran to the bathroom and stared at her reflection in the mirror. She looked ghastly. Her eyes were red-rimmed from crying, with black mascara-circles smudged under her eyes. Her nose was running and as red as Rudolph's. Too weary to style her hair this morning, she had tied it back in a makeshift ponytail. It looked hideous. With rising panic, she let her hair down and fluffed it with her fingers, but now it stuck out oddly, making her look like some crazy creature in a horror flick.

She couldn't let Jeff see her like this, especially if this was going to be their last time together. If he was leaving her forever, she at least wanted him to carry away a pleasing last impression of her.

But where to begin? He said he was on his way over. How much time did that give her? Five minutes? Ten? Or what if he had called while he was actually en route? He could arrive at any second.

Marnie washed off the mascara, but she couldn't do anything about her red, swollen eyes. Jeff would know she had been crying, and that was the last thing she wanted. He had made his decision to go, and that was that. Let him go. She didn't want his pity.

As she ran a brush through her tangled hair, the doorbell rang. She looked down at her oversized tee and sweatpants. She wished she could change into something more feminine, but there was no time.

She hurried to the door, paused to catch her breath, then opened it, praying that she looked more calm, cool, and collected than she felt. "Hi, Jeff," she said, trying to sound nonchalant.

"Hi, Marnie." He looked a little nervous and unsure of

himself. "Can I come in a minute?"

"Sure." She stepped aside.

He entered, rubbing his hands together as if debating what to say. "I won't take much of your time, Marnie."

"That's okay. I'm not going anywhere."

"Can we sit down?"

"I guess." They took opposite ends of the sofa.

He gave her a closer look. "Are you feeling okay?"

She looked away, but there was nowhere to hide. "Yeah. Why?"

"You look like you're coming down with a cold."

"It's nothing. My allergies must be kicking up."

"You don't have allergies."

"Whatever." Why did he have to catch her looking like this? It was bad enough that their relationship was ending. At least she should have been able to say good-bye to him with her hair styled, her makeup on, and her pride intact.

He was still rubbing his hands together. "I have some news, Marnie."

She nodded. "You're going to Cambodia."

He looked startled, taken aback. "How did you know?"

"Jen told me. Nate told her."

"News travels fast."

"Not as fast as your travel plans."

He sat back and drew in a deep breath. "I found out about the opening on the ministry team when I got home last night. Then, this morning, everything just fell into place. I was able to sign up, do all the necessary paperwork, and get a plane ticket. I even squeezed in time to take my last two finals. It just seems like the Lord orchestrated the whole thing."

"How long will you be gone?"

"Two months. I'll be back in time for fall classes." He shifted, turning to face her. "We'll be flying in to Phnom Penh. From there, we'll drive north to do some prison ministry at the maximum-security prison in Ratanakiri. Then, we'll travel south through Stung Treng and Kompong Cham back to Phnom Penh. Do you remember any of those places?"

"No. Should I?"

"We held Bible classes for the children in Kompong Cham. In that box in the cupboard are some photos of us holding the kids. They loved you. They were always flocking around you, wanting you to pick them up. I'm sorry we didn't get to see those pictures last night."

She looked away, tears starting in her eyes. "Me, too."

"Anyway, besides evangelistic meetings, our team will be holding discipleship classes for Christian teens. We're teaching them to minister to their own people. Did you know 80 percent of Cambodians are under the age of thirty?"

"No, I didn't know." Why was he rambling on about everything except what was on both of their minds—the final death throes of their marriage? Gazing down at her hands, she pushed back the cuticle of her thumbnail until it hurt. "So, is that all you came over to say?"

He sat forward and massaged his knuckles. "I came to pick up the rest of my things. I don't have much here—my guitar, a few clothes, some books and papers. I assume you won't still be in Hawaii when I get back from Cambodia."

The casual way he remarked that she wouldn't be here made her wince inside. Plus, her cuticle was bleeding now. She wanted to say, *How do you know where I'll be?* But he was right. She wouldn't be here in the fall. "I'm going home to Michigan in a few days."

"That's what I figured." He cracked his knuckles—first one hand and then the other. "Listen, Marnie. I want you to know I'm not going to stop you if you want to file for an annulment."

Fresh tears filled her eyes, but she turned away so he wouldn't notice.

"Did you hear me, Marnie?"

She blinked rapidly. "Yes, I heard you. Fine. I'll look into it."

He stood up. "I'll go get my stuff."

While he gathered his belongings, she busied herself in the kitchen—washing the same dish over and over. Silently she prayed, *Help me, Lord! I don't know what to do. I don't know what to say. Just when I saw a glimmer of hope for Jeff and me, it's all falling apart. How did things get so bad between us?*

After a while, he came out with his guitar over his shoulder and a duffel bag in each hand. "There are still a few things left." He set his bags by the door. "The rent is paid until the end of the month. Nate will stop by and get the rest of my junk before you leave."

"Okay."

"I'm sorry I won't be able to help you pack up this place. Maybe Nate can round up some of the guys and help you out—you know, packing, cleaning the floors, stuff like that."

Marnie hadn't thought that far ahead. All the pieces of her life were here in this apartment. How was she possibly going to box it all up and take it back to Michigan? "If I need help, I'll call Nate."

"Do that. I don't want you trying to do it all yourself. You're not that strong yet."

"I'm strong enough," she said defensively.

He managed a grim smile. "Yeah, maybe you are." He opened the door then turned back to her. "If you need anything, Marnie—anything at all. . ." His voice trailed off.

"I'm fine," she said, while a little voice in her head screamed, *I'm anything but fine!*

He nodded. "Great."

There was that word again—*their* word.

"Yeah. Great," she repeated.

They stood staring at each other for a long while, neither speaking. Marnie could see the emotion playing out in Jeff's eyes and in the way he flexed his lips, as if he were about to say something and then changed his mind.

Her own heart was crying out, *Let's go back and erase last night and start over. Let's figure out how we can have the kind of love God talks about in the Bible.* But she couldn't bring herself to say the words aloud.

"Marnie—" Jeff clasped her arm. "You take care of yourself, okay? When you go home to Michigan, keep up your therapy and do what the doctor tells you."

She nodded. "My mom will see to that."

"Great. I love that about your mom." He leaned over and kissed her cheek, like a brother would. "You'll always be in my prayers, Marnie."

"Thanks." She licked her dry lips. "You'll be in mine, too."

He glanced around the room as if he didn't know quite what to do next. She followed his gaze, knowing he was remembering the times they had spent together in this apartment—the good times and bad. Finally, he looked back at her, his eyes glazed with unshed tears. It was all she could do to keep herself from rushing into his arms and begging him to stay. But that would be cruel and selfish of her. As much as she wanted to work things out with him right now, tomorrow, she might be pushing him away again, afraid to be the wife he needed. It wasn't fair to keep him on an emotional roller-coaster ride. Besides, Jeff had made his decision. His heart belonged to the missions. She had no right to keep him here when God was calling him to Cambodia.

"We had some special times here," he murmured. "I'll never forget that."

"Me neither." But that was the problem. She had forgotten. The memories were lost forever. And until now, she had been too afraid to build new ones.

Kissing the top of her head, he whispered, "Stay in touch." Then, with a sigh, he opened the door, picked up his bags, and strode outside, letting the door clatter behind him.

Even after he had gone, Marnie stood watching the closed door, certain that Jeff would turn around and come back. It couldn't be over as simply as this. At any moment, he would come striding back inside, laughing and telling her he had no intention of going; this was just his way of making her realize how much they meant to each other.

Finally, she pressed her cheek against the door and let the tears flow. Her headache was back, too, more severe than any she had experienced before. But at least the physical pain helped deaden the emotional pain. When all that remained were dry sobs, she went to her room, stretched out on the bed, and let sleep bring its anesthetizing solace.

Marnie's first thought when she woke the next morning was that Jeff would be flying to Cambodia about the same time she was giving her speech in her ESL class. The thought made her feel even more empty and alone than she had felt last night. Without Jeff, she felt marooned, rudderless. She wanted nothing more than to pull the covers over her head and let slumber obliterate her pain. But that wasn't possible. She had to face the fact that he was gone and she was on her own now.

"But I'm not alone, am I, Lord?" she whispered as she gazed at the sunlight streaming in the window. "You're with me. I can do all things through Christ who strengthens me. Help me to live those words. In my weakness, please show Your strength, Father. I love You, Jesus."

With a prayer on her lips, she forced herself to get out of bed and go about her usual routine of breakfast, devotions, showering, and dressing. She put on her green drawstring top and white denim capris and styled her hair the way Jeff liked— with crimped curls framing her face just so.

She spent the next few hours going over her presentation until it was word perfect. As she grabbed a peanut butter and jelly sandwich for lunch, she realized she'd better phone her mother and let her know she would be coming home next week. Her mom had insisted she stay and try to salvage her marriage, but even her mother couldn't protest her coming home when she learned that Jeff had left for Cambodia.

She managed to get through the first few minutes of their conversation without giving in to her emotions. But when her mother asked how she felt about Jeff's leaving, she burst into tears. "I didn't want him to go, Mom, but I can't blame him. I couldn't be his wife, and he said he doesn't want just a—a buddy."

Her mother's voice came back firm and reassuring. "Listen, honey, I'm not letting you come home alone. Your dad and I will fly over—today if we can get a flight—and help you pack up your apartment. Then we'll bring you home. You just go finish your classes, and I'll call you later with our flight information."

All she could manage to say was "Thanks, Mom." She hadn't mentioned her headaches. Another one was brewing even as they spoke—spiking in her skull like a hot iron striking an anvil. But there was no sense in worrying her mother unnecessarily.

After saying their good-byes, Marnie closed her cell phone, gathered the materials for her presentation, and set off for the campus. It wasn't a long walk, but besides being uphill, the day was warmer and more humid than usual, even for Hawaii.

By the time Marnie walked into her ESL class, she was feeling overheated, lightheaded, and breathless. She sat down in her seat and prayed that her headache would abate long enough for her to give her presentation. She was the second student the instructor called on. As she picked up her notes and walked to the lectern, she prayed that God would help her. Her mind felt fuzzy, her thoughts disjointed. She arranged her notes and gazed out at her fellow classmates.

"My name is Marnie Rockwell—um, I mean, Marnie Jordan, and my topic is. . ." She was having a hard time forming her words correctly. The words on the page blurred, and the faces watching her were suddenly transformed into distorted, dizzying, multiplying shapes. She closed her eyes and gripped the lectern. She was feeling nauseated. Her headache was paralyzing now— her skull about to explode while searing, knifelike pain shot down her neck.

"I'm sorry," she murmured. "I—I can't do this."

Even as she said the words, the world started spinning around her—faces blending, colors meshing, the very room turning topsy-turvy like a carnival ride gone terribly wrong. Trapped in a nightmarish vortex of pain, she felt herself sinking down, down, collapsing into a chasm so dark and deep she might never return.

fifteen

Jeff set his laptop, carry-on bag, shoes, and the contents of his pockets—keys, wallet, cell phone, and change—on the screening table then handed his passport and plane ticket to the security guard. Ahead of him, his team members had already passed through the metal detectors and were collecting their possessions. They had two hours before their plane would be flying them from the small, open-air Kona airport to Honolulu, and then on to Tokyo for a connecting flight to Bangkok, and another connecting flight to Phnom Penh. From there, they would take a van north to Ratanakiri. It would be over twenty-eight hours before they touched down in Cambodia, so he had come prepared with several books and a bag full of snacks—candy bars, chips, beef jerky, and hastily made ham sandwiches.

Just as he was collecting his belongings, his cell phone rang. Striding away from the security checkpoint, he opened the phone and said a hushed hello. It was Nate. "Hey, bro, what's up?" he asked, keeping an eye on his team members up ahead. They were already halfway to the gate, and he was lagging behind, bringing up the rear. "I can't talk now, man. We're heading to our gate. I'll call you back just before we board."

The reception was bad, and when the phone cut out, Jeff wasn't sure he had heard Nate correctly. "What'd you say—what about Marnie?"

"She collapsed in class," said Nate. "They took her to the hospital. She's being prepped for surgery."

Jeff stopped in his tracks and set his bags at his feet. "Surgery? What happened to her?"

"No one knows. But it looks serious, buddy."

Jeff sucked in a breath. He felt as if the wind had been knocked out of him. "Is she gonna be okay?"

"I have no idea," said Nate. "But I figured you'd wanna know."

"Yeah, I sure do. See if you can get some more information, okay?"

He hung up the phone, his head spinning with questions. What could have happened to Marnie? She was fine last night—except for the headaches. *Lord, help her. Take care of my girl. Let her be okay.*

As he joined his team members at the gate, his mind was in a tailspin. He set his stuff on a chair and turned to Charles, the team leader. "I got a problem," he said, his thoughts running blindly. How could he explain what he himself didn't know?

"What is it, Jeff?" Charles—a big-boned, red-faced Swede with wispy blond hair—had a way of sounding calm and reassuring, no matter what was happening around him.

Jeff needed a little of that composure right now. "It's my wife," he said, his voice catching. "She's in the hospital."

Compassion registered in Charles's eyes. "What can we do for her?"

Jeff was on the verge of tears. The last thing he wanted was to look like a crybaby in front of the guys. "That's just it. I don't know what's wrong. It could be serious."

Charles clasped Jeff's shoulder. "Let's pray for her right now, man." He called the other guys over, and they formed a circle around Jeff. "Heavenly Father," said Charles in his deep, thickly accented voice, "put Your loving arms of protection around Marnie this very minute. We don't know what's wrong, Lord, but You do, and we entrust her to Your care. And give Jeff Your comfort and courage. Help him to know what he needs to do right now."

As they all said, "Amen," Jeff had to steel himself to keep from bawling. He swiped at a tear and spoke over a lump in his throat. "Listen, guys, I don't know how to say this, but I can't go to Cambodia with you. Marnie's my wife, and I've gotta stay here by her side."

Charles shook his hand heartily. "You go take care of your wife, Jeff. We'll trust God to pick up the slack for us. It's His ministry. He's in charge."

Grabbing his bags, Jeff nearly sprinted across the airport to a waiting taxi. "Take me to Kona Community Hospital," he said breathlessly. During the drive, he called Nate back and asked if he had any more information. He didn't, but he was phoning classmates and asking them to pray.

Then Jeff phoned Jenny. "Have you heard about Marnie?" he said, the emotion raw in his voice.

"Yes. I heard she was taken to the hospital. What happened, Jeff?"

"I don't know, Jen. I'm on my way to the hospital now."

"Me, too. I called the church and talked to Pastor Maluhia. He's notifying the prayer chain."

"Good. I'll see you in a few minutes."

When the taxi pulled up at the hospital, Jeff jumped out and nearly forgot his luggage. "Hey, man, don't forget your stuff!" called the driver. Returning to the cab, Jeff thrust several dollars into the man's hand and asked him to drop his bags off at his dormitory at U of N.

Every nerve ending bristled as Jeff ran into the hospital and crossed the lobby. "My wife was brought here to the hospital," he told the woman at the information desk. "Her name's Marnie. Marnie Jordan." He was panting so hard he wasn't sure the woman understood him.

Checking her records, she said, "Your wife has been taken to the surgical suite, Mr. Jordan."

Jeff paced the floor. "Why? What happened? What's wrong with her?"

"You'll have to talk with her doctor."

"Where is he?"

"I'll page him, but he may already be in the operating room.

We have some papers for you to sign, Mr. Jordan—permission forms for surgery, since you're her closest relative. Then you may wait for Dr. Forlani in the visitors' lounge."

Jeff signed the forms, but there was no way he was going to sit around waiting for news. He had spent a lot of time in this hospital when he and Marnie were recuperating from the accident. He knew half the nurses on the staff. Now he just had to find one who would give him some answers.

It didn't take him long. He found a surgical nurse named Elena on duty in the emergency room. She greeted Jeff with a big hug. "I'm so relieved you're here, Mr. Jordan. You and your wife were always my favorite patients."

"How's Marnie?" he asked.

The woman's expression darkened. "I was here when they brought her in. She was unconscious. They ran tests—a CT scan, MRI, and ultrasound. I believe they've taken her to surgery."

"What's wrong with her?"

She hesitated. Jeff could see the indecision playing in her olive black eyes. "I should wait and let the doctor tell you."

"Please, Elena—!" He clasped her arm. "I've got to know."

"They—they suspect a ruptured cerebral aneurysm."

Jeff caught his breath. "That's bad, isn't it?"

"It can be."

"People die of those!"

"Yes, but they're acting quickly. We must trust they've caught it in time."

"She was having headaches," said Jeff. "I should have recognized the signs. If anything happens to her. . ."

"You can't blame yourself, Mr. Jordan."

"Why not? She needed me, and I wasn't here."

"You're here now. That's what counts."

"I've got to see her."

"I don't know if that's possible now."

"Jeff!"

He looked around. It was Jenny. She came running up to him, her brown hair flying, her dark eyes filled with concern. "How is she? Do you know anything?"

"They said she might have—" He could hardly get out the words. "She might have an aneurysm, Jen. They've taken her to surgery."

"Why don't you both sit down," said Elena, "and I'll go see if there's any news. Maybe Dr. Forlani hasn't scrubbed yet."

They walked over to the visitors' lounge and sat down on wicker chairs. "What do you know about aneurysms?" Jeff asked Jenny.

"Not much. Isn't it when an artery bulges out like a balloon?"

He nodded. "And if it bursts, it can kill you."

Jenny put her hand over his. "Everyone's praying for her. Students all over campus are setting up little prayer groups."

"But what if God wants to take her home?" He pummeled his fist against his palm. "She's gone through so much already this year, Jen. And now this!"

"She's in God's hands, Jeff. There's no better place to be."

The brisk click of leather shoes on the tile floor caught Jeff's attention. He looked up to see Dr. Forlani striding toward him in his surgical gown. The doctor greeted him with a solemn nod and shook his hand. "Mr. Jordan—Jeffrey—we need to talk. Will you join me in the consultation room?"

"What about Marnie? Is she okay?"

"Come with me."

Jeff gave Jenny a helpless shrug and followed Dr. Forlani to a small room just off the visitors' lounge. The surgeon sat down at a small oak desk; Jeff settled into an overstuffed chair. His heart was pounding so hard he wondered if he'd be able to hear or comprehend the doctor's words.

Dr. Forlani sat forward, folded his hands, and got right to the point. "Jeffrey, we've just completed several tests, including an angiogram, on your wife. They show that an aneurysm has ruptured in her brain at the intersection of her ophthalmic artery and one of her carotid arteries. It may be the result of trauma from her accident last January. Whatever the cause, blood is spilling into surrounding brain tissue and, without treatment, will likely lead to a host of problems."

"What problems? Don't dance around it, Doctor. Tell me the truth."

"Without proper treatment, Marnie may suffer brain damage, paralysis, or a stroke. She could go into another coma and never wake up. She could die."

Jeff's stomach knotted. He was going to be sick. "You've got to save her, Doctor."

"We'll do everything we can. We need your permission to operate."

"I know. I already signed the papers."

"Good. Then there's something else we need to talk about. We have two options. The traditional approach is a craniotomy. The procedure is known as microvascular clipping. We remove a section of the skull and clip off the aneurysm to stop the bleeding."

Jeff shook his head. "Marnie's already had brain surgery. I don't know if she could survive it again."

Dr. Forlani cleared his throat. "The other option eliminates invasive surgery. It's a newer technique called endovascular coiling. A catheter is guided up through the patient's groin into the ruptured blood vessel. Then tiny platinum coils are deployed into the aneurysm to make the blood clot and create a seal."

"That sounds better than drilling into her skull," said Jeff. "Do that one."

"Here's the problem. As a neurosurgeon, I can perform the craniotomy immediately. If you want the noninvasive coiling, we need an interventional radiologist."

"Then get one." Jeff's impatience was growing. Why was Dr. Forlani wasting time talking and throwing around all these tongue-twisting terms? "Do whatever's best for Marnie."

"The closest interventional radiologist is Dr. Iwamoto, in Honolulu," said Dr. Forlani. "I've already contacted him, and he's flying to Kona even as we speak."

"Great. Then he'll be able to fix Marnie's head."

"Here's the dilemma, Jeffrey." Dr. Forlani leaned forward with a quiet, confidential air. "While the coiling method is less risky and offers a much shorter recovery time, your wife's condition could deteriorate while we wait for Dr. Iwamoto to arrive. As I said, Marnie could suffer a stroke. She could die before we have a chance to treat her."

Jeff felt what little strength and composure he had drain right out of him. "Then do the other one—the cranio—"

"Craniotomy. But the risk there is that Marnie might not be strong enough to survive the surgery."

"Then what do we do?" Jeff's voice came out sounding shrill and desperate.

"I suggest we wait for Dr. Iwamoto. He will be able to determine which procedure is best for Marnie. But if you don't choose to wait, I will go ahead with the craniotomy."

Jeff sat back, closed his eyes, and cupped his hands behind his neck. "Lord, I feel like I'm holding Marnie's life in my hands. What do You want me to do?" Tears welled in his eyes. His mouth felt as dry as sand. He could hardly get out the words. "I don't want anyone cutting into Marnie's head again. We'll wait for Dr. Iwamoto."

For Jeff, the next few hours were a blur. Dozens of his classmates joined him in the visitors' lounge and took turns praying for Marnie. Two hours passed before Dr. Iwamoto arrived from Honolulu, and then another hour crept by before the surgeons confirmed they were going with the minimally invasive coiling treatment.

Just before the orderlies wheeled Marnie into the operating room, Dr. Forlani allowed Jeff a few minutes with her. He entered her room with fear and trembling. What would he find? How bad would it be? Seeing her, he uttered a wistful sigh. She was still his Marnie, the girl he adored. She looked like a sleeping princess. Or like a fragile china doll lying so quiet and still in the large hospital bed.

She wasn't aware of his presence, but he sat down, took her hand, and prayed over her. "Father, she's in Your hands now. Take care of her. Please let her be okay." After he had prayed, he got up, leaned over, and kissed her forehead. "I hope we made the right choice for you, Marnie. Please come back to me. I love you so much." The words spilled out between broken sobs. "And I promise—I'll never leave you again—no matter what."

For the next two hours, he sat in the visitors' lounge with Jenny and Nate and all the others from the church and university who had gathered to show their support. As he waited and prayed, he received a phone call from Marnie's parents. Their plane had arrived in Kona—they had come to take their daughter home to Michigan—and they were worried that she wasn't answering her cell phone.

"I tried to reach you," said Jeff, "but I guess you were already in the air." With halting words, he told them about Marnie's aneurysm and tried to reassure them that she was getting the best of care. They stayed on the line with him, urging him to relate every detail while they flagged a cab and headed for the hospital.

They arrived twenty minutes later, worried and exhausted and full of questions. It was irrational, but somehow Jeff felt as if he had let them down—he hadn't taken care of their daughter the way he had promised. He was too emotionally spent to go through the motions of introducing Marnie's parents to everyone, but, to his relief, his friends quickly gathered around and welcomed them. Many remembered the Rockwells from their previous visits after Jeff and Marnie's accident. There was a lot of hugging and weeping and muffled words of comfort.

For Jeff, all the commotion was too much, considering at this very moment Marnie's life hung in the balance. He couldn't handle other people's emotions and neediness right now. He sat forward and buried his face in his hands. If the doctors didn't come with news soon, he was going to explode. If only he could get away by himself and sit in silence and pray.

He was relieved when Jenny put her hand on his shoulder and said, "Jeff, why don't you go get some fresh air. I'll keep Mr. and Mrs. Rockwell company."

He gave her a look that said, *Thank you, thank you!* Aloud he said, "Are you sure?"

"More than sure. Take a little break."

Nate joined in and said, "Hey, bro, I'll come get you if there's any news." Turning to the Rockwells, Nate said, "I'd be glad to go get you two some coffee or bring you back something from the cafeteria if you're hungry."

"Coffee would be good," said Barbara, wiping away a tear, "but we're not moving from here until we know our daughter's okay."

"Excuse me. I'll be right back." Before anyone could say another word, Jeff was on his feet and striding down the hall. Maybe he was being a coward for not wanting to deal with other people's pain, but right now, he was feeling spiritually depleted. He needed a touch from the Lord more at this moment than he ever had in his life. He kept walking until he was outside the hospital.

It surprised him to see that it was dark already. The sky was a deep azure blue, the air still heavy with the heat of the day and the wafting fragrance of bougainvillea. He crossed the thick grass and found a private spot around the corner of the building. Leaning against the wall, he put his head back and wailed. The sound that escaped his lips shocked him. It was more than a moan; it was a deep, guttural lament—primal and raw. He wept, his chest heaving with sobs until there was nothing left.

"Lord," he whispered at last, "no matter what happens, I'm Yours. Marnie is Yours. It's all in Your hands. I give it all to

You, Father. I'm holding nothing back. Do what You will. Just don't let us go. Keep us always in Your arms. I love You, Jesus. I'll always love You."

He wiped away his tears, blew his nose, and, after composing himself, went back inside. He felt like he'd just been through the biggest workout of his life. He was physically spent but spiritually stronger. He had connected with the Holy Spirit in a way he couldn't even define with words. God was with Him. He could face anything now.

Returning to the visitors' lounge, he spotted Dr. Forlani talking with the Rockwells. *He's giving them news about Marnie, and I wasn't even here!* After sidestepping a table and nearly colliding with a passing nurse, he joined them, his heart pumping like crazy. He looked the doctor straight in the eye. "How's Marnie?"

Dr. Forlani's small dark eyes were hard to read. "The procedure was successful. I was just telling Mr. and Mrs. Rockwell that Dr. Iwamoto did an excellent job. He was able to identify the aneurysm and fill it with coils of platinum wire. The coils will mesh together, causing the blood to clot and form a seal. We're pleased that we were able to accomplish our goal without highly invasive surgery."

Jeff's hopes soared. "Then Marnie's going to be okay?"

Dr. Forlani raised his hand in a cautionary gesture. "She's not out of the woods yet, Jeffrey. She'll be in intensive care for the next twenty-four hours. There's still the danger of bleeding and of spasms in the blood vessels causing a stroke. We'll be monitoring Marnie's vital signs constantly, and we have her on a heart monitor to watch for abnormal heart rhythms. But if Marnie's recovery progresses as well as Dr. Iwamoto's coil embolization procedure, then I predict you'll have your wife back in your arms in a matter of days."

sixteen

She was standing in the midst of a green valley that stretched as far as the eye could see. The color was startling in its intensity— a bright emerald green nearly blinding to the eyes. Purple mountains with a soft velvet sheen surrounded the valley like cardboard cutouts pasted against a pastel blue sky studded with puffball clouds.

She was walking barefoot through tall grass that rustled against her bare legs. Where she walked, the crushed tendrils exuded a fresh, verdant scent. The breeze that kissed her face carried the fragrance of roses and the song of birds soaring overhead. Music played in the air like the patter of raindrops and the flutter of angel wings. It was a beautiful valley—as timeless and entrancing as it was peaceful.

Still, the journey was endless as she forced one foot ahead of the other through thick, clinging brush. The more she walked, the longer the distance grew to the other side of the valley. At times, the sun peeked through the clouds and shot out its blinding rays in little explosions of sheer, pure white. She covered her eyes, but the light kept growing, finally obliterating everything around her.

Weariness was about to consume her when a hand reached out and touched her shoulder. She grasped the willing fingers and held on for dear life. As loving arms embraced her, she felt warmth that transcended physical comfort. She wasn't alone anymore. Someone was with her, holding her close.

Someone else followed her as well—a shadowy figure lingering nearby, whispering words of hope and reassurance. "Marnie, I love you, sweetheart. You're going to be okay."

Of course she was going to be okay. She had this valley. She had never felt more at peace. This valley was taking her home. It was a long, hard journey, but she would get there someday.

"Marnie, can you hear me?"

The voice was familiar. As she turned her face toward it, the valley ebbed away. The music was gone; in its place, a jarring cacophony of noises. The wafting fragrance of roses had given way to an assault of repugnant, antiseptic smells. Everything about the world was suddenly crass and harsh and out of sync with her valley. She opened her eyes as if to ask, *Why did you disturb me? Why did you bring me back to. . .this?*

"Marnie, it's me—Jeff."

"Hi. . .Jeff." Her mouth felt cottony and tasted as stale as week-old chewing gum. Every part of her body was waking to stiffness and discomfort. "Where am I?"

"In the hospital. Do you remember what happened?"

"No." She turned her head away. Somehow, whatever it took, she had to get back to the green valley. But it was too late. It was already a fleeting memory. She was here now, in a sterile hospital room, trapped once again by a ruthless reality that demanded she fight her way back to normalcy. "I thought I was dead," she murmured.

Jeff placed his palm over her forehead. "We wouldn't let you go. God answered our prayers and brought you back to us."

"I'm not. . .back yet." She closed her eyes and let sleep enfold her.

For Marnie, the next few days were a broken mosaic of disrupted slumber, disjointed dreams, and faceless nurses coming and going like silent apparitions, murmuring singsong words that came at her from a distance.

And then one morning, she awoke in her hospital room and realized she felt alive again, almost normal. The headaches were gone, replaced by a sprig of hope in her soul. Whatever had happened, whatever dark, troubling journey she had just come through, God was with her, giving her another chance at life.

She opened her eyes and looked around. Jeff was sitting by

her bed in an overstuffed chair, his chin on his chest, sleeping.

"Wake up. . .sleepyhead." Her voice came out husky, hardly there.

But Jeff heard. He sat bolt upright and stared at her. "Marnie, did you just say something?"

"Wake up."

He jumped to his feet. "That's what I thought you said."

She managed a faint half smile. "You're. . .sleeping on the job."

He grinned sheepishly. "Sorry, babe. I just dozed off."

"I need. . .water."

He brought over her glass and held the straw while she sipped, his eyes full of wonder and concern. "How are you, sweetheart?"

She searched his eyes. He really had a rather handsome face. "You tell me."

Sitting down on the edge of the bed, he took her hand and rubbed the back of it with his thumb. "Dr. Forlani says you're going to be fine. You'll need to be on medication for a while, but that's no big deal."

Her mind was still fuzzy. "What happened to me?"

"What's the last thing you remember?"

She thought a minute. The images in her mind were jumbled, out of focus. "I was going to my ESL class. I had to give a presentation."

"It didn't happen, babe."

"Why not? I worked so hard on it."

"You collapsed. They had to take you to the hospital."

"I don't remember."

"Do you remember me?"

"Of course. You're Jack."

He smacked his forehead. "Oh no, not again!"

Marnie started giggling. "I'm only kidding. You're Jeff. My husband."

"Whew! You know how to scare a guy."

"Did you really think I didn't know you?"

"Yeah. I figured you considered me some stranger off the street again."

She shook her head. "No way." She paused for a long moment, trying to gather her thoughts. "So, Jeff, are you going to tell me why I'm here?"

"Sure, babe. It's a long story, but I'll give you the condensed version." In a few short, matter-of-fact sentences, he told her what had happened. But it was all coming at her too fast. She could make sense of only a few words—aneurysm, surgery, everyone praying.

In alarm, she felt her head then sighed in relief. "I still have my hair."

"Yeah, I wasn't about to let them cut into your head again."

"You told them that?"

"Sort of. I'm your closest relative. I had to give my permission. They asked my opinion, so I told them."

She managed a generous smile this time. "Thank you for looking after me."

He reached over and smoothed back her hair. "I'm just so grateful you're going to be okay, babe. I was so worried. I had to keep turning my fears over to the Lord, but He was there for me all the way."

"He was with me, too." She loved the touch of Jeff's palm on her forehead. His closeness brought back a memory from the green valley of her dreams. "I was in this beautiful place. I kept walking, but I couldn't get to the other side. I wasn't afraid because I wasn't alone. Jesus was beside me, holding me up when I couldn't walk."

"That's a cool dream, Marnie."

"There was someone else with me, too, Jeff."

"Yeah? Who?"

"I think it was you. I couldn't see your face, but I knew it was you."

"Yeah, it was me." He walked his fingers through her hair, gently separating the strands. "I was sitting here by your bed day and night—until they kicked me out and told me to go home and get some sleep."

"How long have I been here?"

"Five days. You'd wake up long enough to complain a little then go back to sleep. The doctor said if you didn't come around pretty soon he was going to kick you out and give someone else your bed."

She eyed him suspiciously. "He didn't say that."

"Okay. He didn't. But he will be glad that you're really back with us—all bright-eyed and bushy-tailed, as my mom used to say."

She gave him a bemused smile. "I don't have a tail."

He grinned. "Okay, we'll skip that part. But your beautiful brown eyes are bright again. That's what counts." He turned and looked toward the closed door. "I'd better get the doctor. He'll want to talk to you. And your parents. They've been camping by your bed as much as I have."

"My mom and dad are here?"

"They sure are. In fact, half the students from U of N have been here at one time or another. And Pastor Maluhia and most of the people from church. You're a pretty popular girl."

"I'm afraid I wasn't much company."

"That's okay. You can make up for it. Just seeing your big smile will do it for most of us."

A thought occurred to her. "Jeff, I just remembered. You were going to Cambodia."

He nodded. "I was at the airport waiting to board the plane when I got news about your collapse. There was no way I was going to leave the country with you sick in the hospital."

She lowered her gaze. She was grateful, but she had no words to express it. Finally, she said, "Thanks for staying with me."

Jeff's eyes glistened. "There's nowhere I'd rather be, Marnie."

She pulled at several frayed threads on her blanket. "Now that I'm better, maybe you can still catch up with your mission team." It was the last thing she wanted, but she hoped she sounded convincing, for Jeff's sake.

"No way." He squared his shoulders and tightened his jaw. "I'm not leaving you again, no matter what you say or do. Even if you never remember our life together, you can't make me go."

"I can't?" Something akin to joy rose in her chest. "But you had your heart set on going overseas with the mission team."

He moved his fingers along her hairline to her earlobe. "The only thing I care about right now is helping you get well and back on your feet."

That was exactly what she wanted to hear. She clasped his hand against her cheek. "I want to go home, Jeff."

He gave her a puzzled look. "You mean to Michigan? You wanna go home with your parents?"

"No, not Michigan. I want to go home with *you*."

A light of comprehension swept across his face. "Are you serious? You mean, back to our apartment? You wanna go home—the two of us together?"

She nodded. "Is it too late?"

"It's never too late."

Relief washed over her. "Jeff, that night when you said you were going away forever, I felt so miserable." The words tumbled out, her voice raspy and weak but full of urgency. "I wanted to run after you and beg you to stay. But I was too stubborn and proud. Do you hate me for sending you away?"

"Of course I don't hate you." He was laughing now, his eyes crinkling with merriment. "How could I ever hate you, silly girl?"

She touched his cheek, his chin. "Does this mean you still... love me?"

He gathered her into his arms and pressed her head against his chest. "I never stopped loving you, sweetheart. When I thought you were going to die, I realized just how much I love you."

"I love you, too, Jeff."

The words hung in the air for a full moment—dazzling and dancing and full of promise. He stared at her in astonishment.

"Does this mean you remember our life together—our wedding, our marriage, the love we shared? Do you finally remember *me*, Marnie?"

She gazed up at him, mentally tracing the solid line of his forehead and jaw. "No, Jeff. I'm sorry. I still don't remember the man you were before the accident."

Disappointment glinted in his gentle blue eyes. "I was hoping—"

"Wait, I'm not finished." Her emotions were rising, catching her by surprise, leaving her breathless. "I know only the man you are right now—the man who stayed by my side even when I didn't know you were here. That's the man I love, Jeff. The man I'll always love."

seventeen

A bright orange sun hovered over the crystal waters and salt-and-pepper sand of Kahaluu Beach as Marnie stepped from the pavilion in her *holoku*—a Hawaiian A-line satin gown with a ruffled train, hand-beaded with lace and sequins. Placing the *haku* orchid lei on Marnie's crimped curls, her mother smiled her approval. "You look breathtaking, honey."

"Thanks, Mom. At least my wedding dress still fits."

Her mother clasped her hand. "Are you nervous?"

"Nervous? Look at her, Mrs. Rockwell." Jenny, in her ankle-length taffeta bridesmaid dress, adjusted a white orchid in Marnie's bouquet and handed it to her. "She's absolutely radiant."

"Actually, I am a little nervous," Marnie admitted. "Are you sure I've done this before?" She glanced across the beach at the white, orchid-draped canopy under which dozens of her family and friends sat in plastic chairs waiting for the ceremony to begin. By a jagged outcropping of lava rocks, Jeff and his groomsmen stood talking with Pastor Maluhia. Several ladies from the church, dressed in festive, floral-print silk and organza dresses, were placing glass bowls with orchid blossoms on the buffet tables in the thatched-roof serving area. Musicians were already strumming their guitars and ukuleles in the shade of banyan and plumeria trees and rainbow eucalyptus. In the distance, coconut palms were silhouetted against a vibrant rainbow sky. "I can't remember, Mom. Was I nervous the first time I married Jeff?"

"As nervous as any new bride," said her mother.

"I'm a new bride *now*," said Marnie. "I have no memory of being with Jeff as his wife, so it's as if I'm marrying him for the first time."

Her mother straightened Marnie's train, fanning it out behind her on the loose-packed sand. "I admire Jeff for being willing to wait for you and staying in campus housing until your wedding today."

Jenny, looking as perky as her nickname, smiled at Marnie. "Nate says Jeff's chomping at the bit to carry you across the threshold of your little rose-covered cottage. You have one eager groom there."

Marnie felt her cheeks grow warm. Was she blushing, or was it just Hawaii's tropical heat bringing perspiration to her forehead? It wouldn't be proper to confess that she was nearly as eager as Jeff to start their honeymoon.

Her mother blotted Marnie's face with her lacy handkerchief. "We don't want your makeup to run in this heat."

"It is warm today," said Jenny, "but the air will turn cool once the sun has set."

"Is everything ready?" asked Marnie. "I feel like we're forgetting something."

"Everyone's here," her mother assured her. "All the guests are seated. The musicians are playing. I just checked, and the ladies from your church have done a beautiful job with the buffet. It's an authentic Hawaiian feast—lomi lomi salmon, Kalua pork, fresh pineapple, passion fruit, chicken crepes, mango quiche, rice pilaf." She paused. "Let's see, I've forgotten something. Oh yes. Shrimp dumplings and coconut chutney. Sure different from the wedding dinners in Michigan."

Marnie shook her head. "I can't even think about food right now, Mom."

Leaning close, her mother said, "Take my word for it, sweetheart. After the wedding, your nervousness will vanish and you'll be starved." Confidentially, she added, "Your father has already sampled the jumbo shrimp and teriyaki beef skewers. He says they're out of this world."

"I'll keep that in mind," said Marnie drily.

Jenny pointed at the horizon. "Look, everyone. The sky is already glorious with color. It's going to be a beautiful evening."

"Indeed it is!" Marnie's father came striding toward them looking debonair in his white dinner jacket. "Have you noticed, Barbara? The sky looks like some painter got carried away with his palette."

Marnie chuckled. "Speaking of wild colors, Daddy, you've got a red streak on your chin."

His hand flew to his face. "Uh-oh. Must be the red sauce from the shrimp."

Marnie took her mother's hanky and wiped off the smear. "You stay away from the buffet table, Daddy, until after the wedding."

His brows furrowed. "I just wanted to make sure everything was up to snuff."

"And was it?" Marnie asked with a bemused smile.

"Sure enough. Best wedding buffet I ever saw—or tasted." He turned to Marnie's mother. "But I was talking about this Hawaiian sky. Look at it. I never saw so many colors. I bet you've been so busy you haven't even noticed."

"How could I not notice, Dan?" said her mother, finding a spot of sauce Marnie had missed and dabbing at it with her hanky. "The closest thing we have in Michigan is the northern lights."

Her father waved his wife away. "Leave me alone, Barb. My chin is perfectly clean, thank you."

"No more samples," she warned. "You might spill something on Marnie's gown."

"Look at your mother, Marnie. She's not happy unless she has something to worry about." He tucked her arm in his. "Well, sweet daughter, are you ready to walk down the aisle to your groom?"

"Yes, Daddy." She leaned over and kissed his cheek. "I'm just glad I can hold on to you when my ankles wobble."

"Mine are wobbling, too, on this uneven sand," he confided as they joined the rest of the wedding party at the back of the festive, open-air tent. At the front, Jeff and his groomsmen stood with the pastor beside an orchid-draped arch.

This is it, Marnie acknowledged silently. *A wedding day I'll always remember. After all these months, I'll finally feel like Jeff's wife.*

A woman in a flowing organza dress stepped forward and blew on a conch shell in four directions; the deep, haunting sound echoed on the gentle ocean breeze. As the musicians' tempo picked up with a contemporary love song, Marnie's father escorted her to the front and placed her hand in Jeff's. He looked more handsome than she had ever seen him in his white, long-sleeved aloha shirt and white linen trousers.

Pastor Maluhia stepped forward and asked them to face each other for the exchange of leis. Holding up his right hand, he declared, "*Ei-Ah Eha-No. Ka Malohia Oh Na Lani. Mea A-Ku A-Pau. . . .* May blessings from above rest upon you and remain with you now and forever."

He held up two orchid leis. "Like the rings you exchange, leis are a circle representing an eternal commitment and undying devotion to each other." He handed them each a lei. Jeff placed his around Marnie's neck and kissed her on the cheek. Marnie placed her lei around Jeff's neck and kissed him, too.

"Jeffrey and Marnie, you are renewing your vows surrounded

by God's beauty," said Pastor Maluhia, "the beauty of the land, of the ocean, and of the mountains. You are surrounded also by your *ohana*—your circle of family and friends. May the act of giving and receiving leis represent the continual blossoming of your relationship."

As a caressing breeze stirred around them, the pastor opened his large, worn Bible and read 1 Corinthians 13. Then he set the Bible aside. "My dear friends, Jeff and Marnie have learned the truth of this beautiful love chapter. They have overcome more trials in their brief marriage than most couples face in fifty years. Theirs is a beautiful love story. God has blessed them with a love that has survived incredible odds. Jeffrey has won the woman of his dreams not just once, but twice in a lifetime." He turned to Jeff. "Now we will have the exchange of vows. Jeffrey, please share your heart with Marnie."

Marnie gave her bouquet to Jenny. Jeff clasped her slim hands between his sturdy palms. His strong, sculpted face was dotted with perspiration. His blue eyes reflected the crystal blue of the sea and sky. A tendon along his jaw moved up and down as he said her name. "Marnie, I fell in love with you the first time I saw you on campus at U of N. My love for you deepened when we became friends during our trip to Cambodia. When you married me last summer, I was the happiest man on earth."

He paused and inhaled deeply. "But it wasn't until after our car accident last January that I learned what true love is all about. When I thought you were going to die, I would have given my life for you. When I realized you had no memory of me or our marriage, I was devastated. But I knew you were worth waiting for. I knew, for better or worse, God had brought us together and would work all things out according to His will.

"It was your mom who helped me realize I should concentrate on the future, not the past. Your mom encouraged me to court you as if we had just met. And I am so thankful to God that He helped you come to love me again. I was a pretty clueless, naive guy when we married the first time. But this time, with

God's help, I'm ready to be the husband you need for the rest of our lives, no matter what." He smiled, his blue eyes warming her heart and yet sending a little chill up her spine. "I love you, Marnie."

"I love you, too," she whispered back. Now it was her turn. Her hands trembled slightly in Jeff's warm palms. She let herself be drawn into the depths of his adoring eyes. "Jeff, you are an awesome, godly man. When I was sick and unlovable and pushing you away, you held on to me and wouldn't let me go. You were a kind and gentle stranger drawing me back to God and back to you. You showed me unconditional, Christlike love. You helped me reclaim my faith and begin discovering the person I was before the accident. It's no wonder I fell in love with you the first time. I'm sorry I don't remember the man you were then. But I know the man you are now. And I have fallen in love with you all over again. I take you as my husband, my partner, my lover, and my best friend to love and cherish forever."

With a tear rolling down his cheek, Jeff whispered, "Thank you, babe."

Pastor Maluhia held up his hand in a gesture of benediction. "Dear friends, let us pray." After offering a brief prayer of commitment, he gave a hearty "Amen" and announced, "Jeffrey and Marnie Jordan, by the authority entrusted to me by the State of Hawaii, I now reconfirm that you are husband and wife. Jeff, you may kiss your bride."

He swept Marnie into his arms and kissed her soundly. She returned the kiss. It was sweet and tender and full of promise. For the first time in a long while, she knew she was exactly where she was meant to be. She was with the man she loved. She was home.

epilogue

Two years later. . .

Marnie and Jeffrey Jordan
invite you to share their joy
as they welcome their son
Daniel Gerald Jordan
into their family

Born: June 25 at 3:06 p.m.

Weight: 7 pounds 14 ounces

Length: 21 inches

Who Daniel looks like:
He has his dad's blue eyes
and his mom's reddish brown hair

Where Daniel will reside:
With his parents in
their happy little cottage on the Sangker River
in Battambang, Cambodia

Rejoice with us for all of God's awesome blessings!

A Letter To Our Readers

Dear Reader:

In order that we might better contribute to your reading enjoyment, we would appreciate your taking a few minutes to respond to the following questions. We welcome your comments and read each form and letter we receive. When completed, please return to the following:

Fiction Editor
Heartsong Presents
PO Box 719
Uhrichsville, Ohio 44683

1. Did you enjoy reading *To Love a Gentle Stranger* by Carole Gift Page?
   ❏ Very much! I would like to see more books by this author!
   ❏ Moderately. I would have enjoyed it more if

   _____

   _____

   _____

2. Are you a member of **Heartsong Presents**? ❏ Yes ❏ No
   If no, where did you purchase this book? _____

   _____

3. How would you rate, on a scale from 1 (poor) to 5 (superior), the cover design? _____

4. On a scale from 1 (poor) to 10 (superior), please rate the following elements.

   ____ Heroine   ____ Plot
   ____ Hero   ____ Inspirational theme
   ____ Setting   ____ Secondary characters

5. These characters were special because? _____
_____
_____

6. How has this book inspired your life? _____
_____
_____

7. What settings would you like to see covered in future
   Heartsong Presents books? _____
_____
_____

8. What are some inspirational themes you would like to see
   treated in future books? _____
_____
_____

9. Would you be interested in reading other **Heartsong
   Presents** titles?   ❏ Yes   ❏ No

10. Please check your age range:
     ❏ Under 18   ❏ 18-24
     ❏ 25-34   ❏ 35-45
     ❏ 46-55   ❏ Over 55

Name _____
Occupation _____
Address _____
City, State, Zip _____

Heartsong